THOMAS DEGAN

The Quiet Border

Book 2

Copyright © 2025 by Thomas DeGan

All rights reserved. No part of this publication may be reproduced, stored, or transmitted in any form or by any means, electronic, mechanical, photocopying, recording, scanning, or otherwise without written permission from the publisher. It is illegal to copy this book, post it to a website, or distribute it by any other means without permission.

This novel is entirely a work of fiction. The names, characters, and incidents portrayed in it are the work of the author's imagination. Any resemblance to actual persons, living or dead, events, or localities is entirely coincidental.

Thomas DeGan asserts the moral right to be identified as the author of this work.

Designations used by companies to distinguish their products are often claimed as trademarks. All brand names and product names used in this book and on its cover are trade names, service marks, trademarks, and registered trademarks of their respective owners. The publishers and the book are not associated with any product or vendor mentioned in this book. None of the companies referenced within the book have endorsed the book.

First edition

This book was professionally typeset on Reedsy. Find out more at reedsy.com

1

The Gray Hours

The ruins remembered industry.

Aiyana moved through what had once been a processing facility, her boots finding purchase on concrete slabs split by decades of frost and root. The walls had fallen generations ago, leaving only foundations that traced the shape of extraction: conveyor channels, smelting pits, the rusted bones of machines whose purpose had outlived memory. Moss covered everything in a fur of gray-green, and small trees grew from the floors of roofless rooms. The land was reclaiming what had been taken from it, slowly, patiently, in the way land always did.

Above her, Sitala circled in the pre-dawn dark, invisible against the starless sky. Through their bond, Aiyana felt what the eagle felt: the texture of cold air against feathers, the pull of thermals rising from the warmer ground, the distant glow on the eastern horizon that was not sunrise. That glow was artificial. That glow was their destination.

"Hold at the perimeter," Commander Speaks-Low signed from twenty paces ahead. His gestures were crisp despite two days of travel through rough terrain. The man seemed inexhaustible, though Aiyana had noticed the way he favored his left knee when he thought no one was watching.

The team halted. Five of them in total: Speaks-Low, Aiyana, and three other Sky Guardians whose names she had learned but whose faces she was still memorizing. Talon. River-Runs-Deep. Catches-The-Wind. They had been chosen for this mission because they could move silently, fight decisively, and die without revealing what they knew. That last qualification had not been stated aloud, but everyone understood it.

Aiyana crouched beside a fallen beam, its iron core exposed by rust like bone through rotted flesh. She steadied her breathing and reached for Sitala, deepening the bond until the eagle's senses overlaid her own. The world shifted. Colors muted as motion sharpened. The facility resolved itself against the horizon: a squat complex of concrete and steel, ringed by chain fencing topped with wire that glinted in the floodlights. Guard towers at each corner. A motor pool to the east. The main building sprawled low and wide, like something trying not to be noticed.

Sitala's eyes were better than any technology the Pale Cities had ever built. The eagle counted the guards in the towers. Four visible. Rotating every fifteen minutes, according to the intelligence Elias had provided. The intelligence they were betting their lives on.

Aiyana released the deep bond and returned fully to her own body. The transition left her momentarily dizzy, the world too close and too colorful after seeing through Sitala's vision. She blinked until the ruins around her solidified.

"Report," Speaks-Low signed.

"Four in the towers," Aiyana signed back. "Rotation matches the intel. But the facility is larger than the schematics showed.

There's a western wing that wasn't in the documents."

Speaks-Low's expression did not change, but something shifted in his posture. A tightening. "How much larger?"

"Double, maybe. The new construction looks recent. Months, not years."

He was quiet for a long moment. In that silence, Aiyana heard the distant hum of generators, felt the wrongness of it against the natural quiet of the Frontier. Power here was not grown or harvested. Power here was burned. She could smell the faint petroleum taint on the wind, the signature of the Pale Cities carried across the border like a stain.

"The mission stands," Speaks-Low finally signed. "We adapt."

Aiyana wanted to argue. The mission had been planned around a specific facility layout, specific patrol routes, specific extraction points. An unknown wing meant unknown guards, unknown prisoners, unknown variables that could get them all killed. But she had already made enough trouble on the last mission. Renna was in that facility because of choices Aiyana had made. Speaks-Low was here, risking his life, because Aiyana had been too focused on her own objectives to see the trap closing.

She thought of Nayeli, standing at the edge of a cliff years ago, telling a frightened trainee that readiness was just a story. *The sky does not care about your fears. It only cares about your presence.* Aiyana had stepped off that ledge and learned to fly. She could step into this uncertainty too.

She signed acknowledgment and checked her equipment for the third time. Sky-suit powered and responsive, its organic circuitry warm against her skin like a living thing. Flight membranes folded compact against her forearms. Emergency beacon, disabled for now, because a signal in enemy territory would bring death faster than rescue. The small pouch at her belt containing the access codes Elias had provided, printed on paper that would dissolve in water, in case she was captured, in case everything went wrong.

The codes felt heavier than they should. They were the same hands that had pressed a data chip into her palm in a drainage tunnel beneath Nova-Providence, the same hands she had gripped before leaving him behind. Elias Harren. She remembered his face in the dim light of the Frontier, thinner than the official portraits had suggested, carrying a truth he could no longer keep silent.

He had stayed. She had asked him to come with her, and he had stayed.

In the weeks since, he had continued sending intelligence through the underground networks, messages that traveled by routes she did not fully understand, passed through hands she would never meet. The codes in her pouch had arrived three days ago, accompanied by a note in his careful handwriting: *The facility where they are holding your people. These will get you inside. Be careful.* No signature. No return address. Just the quiet work of a man who had burned his old life to the ground and was building something new from the ashes.

Aiyana did not know if she could still trust him. Not because she doubted his intentions, but because he was deep in enemy territory with enemies who had resources she could not imagine. Had his network been compromised? Had someone fed him false information, knowing it would reach her? The intelligence he had provided about the detention facility matched what they could verify, but verification only went so far.

She knew only that Renna was inside those walls, and Kele too if the reports were accurate, and that she would walk into any trap to bring them home. Trust was a luxury. Necessity was not.

* * *

They approached the facility in two groups.

Speaks-Low took Talon and River-Runs-Deep to the eastern approach, where the motor pool provided cover and the generator noise would mask their movement. Aiyana led Catches-The-Wind toward the western side, toward the new wing, toward the unknown. It was not the original plan. The original plan had her supporting Speaks-Low's team. But if the facility had expanded, someone needed to understand what they were walking into, and Sitala's eyes gave Aiyana advantages the others lacked.

The Frontier here was scarred. Old roads, cracked and overgrown, led toward the Pale Cities like veins toward a heart. The soil was thin, stripped by decades of industrial runoff before the treaties had pushed the border back. Nothing grew tall. The trees were stunted, their leaves pale even in summer. Far to the west, beyond the horizon she could not see, the Wind Spine array would be singing its morning frequencies, Tower Seven's replacement still growing toward the sky. The network compensated for what had been lost, other towers taking the harmonic load, but Aiyana could feel the gap even here, a dissonance in the lower registers that years of training had taught her to recognize.

She wondered if the same was true of people.

Catches-The-Wind moved like his name, silent and unpredictable. He was older than Aiyana by a decade, a veteran of border incidents she had only read about in training. Scars marked his arms where exo-frame claws had found purchase before he had found the pilot's throat. He did not speak much, but when he did, the other Guardians listened.

"There," he signed, pointing toward a drainage culvert that ran beneath the perimeter fence. "Not on the schematics either."

Aiyana studied it through Sitala's distant eyes. The culvert was new construction, concrete still pale where it had not yet weathered. Large enough for a person to crawl through. An oversight in security, or a deliberate trap?

"They expanded fast," she signed. "Faster than they could secure. They're confident no one would come this far."

"Confidence is a weakness."

They waited for the patrol rotation. Sitala tracked the guards in the nearest tower as they handed off to their replacements, the brief moment of distraction as one shift ended and another began. On Catches-The-Wind's signal, they moved.

The culvert was dark and smelled of rust and stagnant water. Aiyana crawled through it on her elbows and knees, her sky-suit's sensors feeding her information she could not see: air quality, temperature gradients, the faint electromagnetic hum of the facility's power grid. MNA technology worked with the body, augmenting senses rather than replacing them. It made her more herself, not less. That was the difference the Pale Cities never understood. Their machines demanded submission. Hers offered partnership.

She emerged inside the perimeter, behind a storage structure that blocked the nearest tower's sightline. Catches-The-Wind followed seconds later, water dripping from his sleeves. They pressed against the cold metal wall and listened.

Voices. Distant, distorted by wind and walls. The clang

of a door. The rumble of a vehicle starting somewhere in the motor pool. Ordinary sounds of a facility going about its business in the gray hours before dawn. They did not know what waited inside those walls. They did not know that a rescue was underway.

Aiyana checked her chronometer. They had forty minutes before the pre-dawn shift change, the window Elias had identified as their best opportunity. Forty minutes to find Renna, find Kele, and extract before the facility fully woke.

It was not enough time. She knew that. Speaks-Low knew that. They were all pretending otherwise because the alternative was leaving their people to rot in Pale City cells.

"Western entrance," she signed. "I'll take point."

Catches-The-Wind nodded once. His hand rested on the weapon at his hip, a compact device that fired concentrated harmonic pulses. Non-lethal, in theory. Theory and practice often diverged when lives were at stake.

They moved.

* * *

The western wing was a detention block.

Aiyana knew it the moment she slipped through the service entrance and saw the corridor stretching ahead: identical doors, each with a small window at eye level, each window reinforced with wire mesh. The air was different here. Recycled, scrubbed of humanity, carrying the faint chemical tang of industrial disinfectant. The lights were too bright, casting no shadows, designed to eliminate any darkness where a prisoner might find comfort.

She had trained for this. She had reviewed the intelligence about Pale City detention practices, the clinical language that described isolation protocols and interrogation techniques.

But training was abstraction. This was real. These walls held people. Some of them might be her people.

Catches-The-Wind covered the corridor behind them while Aiyana approached the first door. The window revealed a small cell, empty, the cot stripped of bedding. She moved to the next. Also empty. And the next.

The fourth cell held a woman. Not MNA. Pale City, by her features and the remnants of civilian clothing. She sat on the floor with her back against the wall, staring at nothing. When Aiyana's shadow crossed the window, the woman did not react. Did not blink. Aiyana moved on.

Elias had said there were other prisoners here. Pale City dissidents, people who had asked the wrong questions or known the wrong truths. The detention facility was not just for enemies of the state. It was for anyone the state found inconvenient. Aiyana filed that knowledge away, another piece of the pattern she was beginning to understand. The Pale Cities were not a monolith. They were fracturing from within, and some of those fractures could be exploited.

But not today. Today was about Renna. Today was about Kele. Today was about the debts Aiyana owed.

She reached the end of the corridor and found a security checkpoint, unmanned at this hour. Beyond it, a second corridor branched left and right. Her chronometer showed thirty-two minutes remaining. Through her bond with Sitala, she sensed the eagle's growing unease, a vibration at the edge of perception that meant something was wrong but not yet wrong enough to name.

"Contact Speaks-Low," she signed to Catches-The-Wind. "We've found the detention block. Western wing. It's bigger than expected."

He activated his communicator, a device grown from organic compounds that transmitted through frequencies the Pale Cities had not learned to monitor. The message would reach Speaks-Low in moments. Whether it would change anything was another matter.

Aiyana chose the left corridor and began checking cells.

More Pale City prisoners. Men and women in institutional gray, some sleeping, some staring, one pacing in tight circles like an animal too long caged. She wondered what they had done. She wondered if any of them had done anything at all, or if suspicion was enough to earn a cell in this place.

The seventh cell stopped her.

The woman inside was not wearing gray. She wore the remnants of an MNA field uniform, torn and stained but unmistakable. Her hair, once long, had been roughly cut. She sat on the cot with her hands folded in her lap, and when Aiyana appeared at the window, she looked up with eyes that held no hope and no surprise.

Renna.

Aiyana's throat tightened. She had imagined this moment a hundred times in the three weeks since the failed summit, since the border closed and the Cold War solidified. She had imagined finding Renna defiant or broken, injured or untouched. She had not imagined this: a stillness that suggested something fundamental had been worn away.

She pulled the access codes from her pouch and entered the sequence on the door's keypad. For a terrible moment nothing happened. Then the lock disengaged with a click that seemed impossibly loud in the silent corridor.

Aiyana stepped inside. The cell smelled of disinfectant and unwashed human. The walls were bare except for scratches near the door frame, marks that might have been counting days.

"Renna," she said, keeping her voice low. "It's Aiyana. We're here to bring you home."

Renna studied her face as though looking for evidence of a trick. Her gaze moved to the doorway, where Catches-The-Wind stood guard. Moved to the open door, the empty corridor beyond. Finally, her expression shifted. Not relief. Something more complex, something Aiyana could not immediately name.

"You shouldn't have come," Renna said. Her voice was rough from disuse. "They know you're here."

Aiyana's blood went cold. "What do you mean?"

"The codes. The ones you used to get in." Renna stood slowly, unfolding limbs that had been still too long. "They gave me those codes. Told me to memorize them. Told me that if anyone used them, it would prove the MNA had an asset inside the city." A ghost of something that might have been a smile crossed her face. "They've been waiting for you, Aiyana. This whole wing is a trap."

Through her bond, Sitala screamed a warning. Footsteps, many of them, converging from multiple directions. The distant wail of an alarm beginning to sound.

Twenty-six minutes left on the chronometer. The window was closing, and the cage was already shut.

Catches-The-Wind appeared in the doorway, his weapon drawn. "Multiple contacts. Eastern approach is compromised."

"Speaks-Low?"

"No word."

Aiyana looked at Renna, at the woman she had come to save, at the bait in a trap that Elias's codes had sprung. But had he known? Had he sent her into this cage deliberately, or had someone intercepted his intelligence, fed him false information because they suspected his loyalties? She remembered his face in the drainage tunnel, the weight of his father's compass in his palm, the way he had said *Stay alive* like it was a prayer.

She could not believe he had betrayed her. But she could believe he had been used.

It didn't matter. Not now.

"Can you move?" she asked Renna.

"I've been waiting three weeks to move."

"Then move. Catches-The-Wind, we're going up."

He understood. Their sky-suits could carry them over the walls, beyond the reach of guards on foot. It meant abandoning the original plan, abandoning the eastern team, abandoning Kele if he was in another part of the facility. It meant survival at the cost of everything else.

"Kele is in the other wing," Renna said, reading Aiyana's hesitation. "He's been there since they separated us. He's..." She stopped. Swallowed. "They've been asking him questions. About the Bioweb. About how it works. He's been trying not to answer."

The alarm was fully sounding now, a harsh electronic wail that echoed through the corridors. The footsteps were closer. Somewhere, a door crashed open.

Aiyana made her choice.

"We get them both," she said. "Catches-The-Wind, take Renna to the extraction point. I'm going for Kele."

"That's not the plan."

"The plan is already dead." She met his eyes, saw the calculation happening behind them. He was weighing her life against the mission, against the information Renna carried, against the cost of losing another Guardian to Pale City cells. "Get her out. I'll find another way."

She did not wait for his answer. She ran.

The corridor blurred around her as she moved, her sky-suit enhancing her speed, her bond with Sitala feeding her information faster than conscious thought. Guards approaching from the north. An exit to the south, currently unblocked. The eastern wing, where Kele waited, separated from her by a security door she did not have codes for.

She would find a way. She always did. That was what Speaks-Low had told her when he agreed to this mission, when he had looked at her with eyes that held no judgment for the failure at the summit. "You find ways, Waketah. It's what you do."

She hoped he was right. She hoped he was still alive to learn whether she succeeded or failed.

The security door loomed ahead, heavy steel reinforced with bars. Beyond it, another world of cells and secrets. Beyond it, Kele. Beyond it, the future she was trying to build or the death she might find instead.

Aiyana pressed her palm against the door and felt the cold of Pale City engineering, the rigid demand of technology that knew nothing of partnership or consent.

Somewhere behind her, she heard voices shouting. Somewhere above her, Sitala circled in the brightening sky, golden feathers catching the first light of dawn.

The door would not open.

But Aiyana had not come this far to be stopped by a door.

She stepped back, activated her sky-suit's emergency protocols, and prepared to make her own entrance.

The alarms screamed. The dawn broke. And somewhere in that fortress of concrete and secrets, Kele was waiting for a rescue that had already become something else entirely.

Aiyana did not know if she would reach him in time. She did not know if any of them would make it home. She knew only that the mission had been compromised from the start, that someone had fed them lies dressed as intelligence, and that the Cold War had just become very, very personal.

She thought of Elias Harren, somewhere in Nova-Providence, perhaps still believing he had helped them. Perhaps already knowing he had not. She thought of his hand in hers, the warmth of his fingers, the way he had squeezed once before letting go. *Stay alive,* she had told him. She wondered if he had.

She thought of Speaks-Low, whose silence on the communicator was becoming a weight she could not ignore.

She thought of Renna's words: *They've been waiting for you.*

The door buckled under the force of her suit's concentrated blast. Steel screamed as hinges tore free. Smoke and debris filled the corridor.

Aiyana stepped through the wreckage into the unknown.

The eastern wing stretched before her, and somewhere in its depths, a man who knew the secrets of the Bioweb was running out of time.

Behind her, the trap closed.

Ahead, something worse was waiting.

2

Static and Silence

The Signal Mesh never slept.

Even here, in a storage room behind a recycling facility where the walls were thick with insulation meant to block transmissions, Elias could hear it. A faint hum at the edge of perception, the electromagnetic pulse of a city talking to itself. Propaganda channels cycling through their overnight programming. Security alerts pinging between stations. The constant murmur of a society that had forgotten what silence sounded like.

He sat with his back against a stack of compressed metal bales, a thin blanket wrapped around his shoulders, and tried to read by the light of a chemical lamp that was slowly dying. The book in his hands was older than his grandfather, its pages brittle and brown at the edges. It had no title on the cover. Titles were dangerous. Titles could be catalogued, tracked, burned.

The text was dense, academic, written in the formal style of historians who had lived before the Doctrine Keepers decided what history meant. Elias had been reading it for three hours, and he still was not certain he understood what he was learning. Only that it contradicted everything.

The Long March, the book called it. The foundational myth of the Pale Cities, the story every child learned before they learned to read. How their ancestors had fled persecution in the eastern lands, had crossed oceans and mountains and deserts, had built a new civilization from nothing in the face of savage opposition. How the Indigenous peoples had tried to destroy them, had waged wars of extermination, had forced the survivors into the industrial enclaves that would become the great cities of Renewal.

Elias had believed it all. Had recited it in school assemblies, had written essays praising the courage of the founders, had felt genuine pride when he walked the streets of Nova-Providence and saw the monuments to those who had sacrificed everything so that he could live free.

The book told a different story.

There had been no persecution. The colonists had come seeking opportunity, and the Indigenous nations had welcomed them under laws of hospitality that predated written memory. Land had been shared. Knowledge had been exchanged. For generations, the newcomers had lived alongside their hosts, learning their languages, adopting their agricultural practices, building communities that blended traditions from both worlds.

Until some of them had decided that sharing was not enough.

The Long March, according to this forbidden history, had not been a flight from persecution. It had been a rejection of integration. A faction of colonists who believed they were destined for dominion, who could not accept living as guests in someone else's home, had gathered their followers and marched east.

Not fleeing savages, but fleeing the expectation that they would remain equal to people they considered inferior.

They had built the Pale Cities not as refuges but as fortresses. Not to protect themselves from Indigenous aggression but to launch their own campaigns of expansion. The wars the Doctrine Keepers called defensive had been wars of conquest. The atrocities they attributed to the Many Nations Alliance had been committed by Pale City forces, then written into history backward.

Elias closed the book and pressed his palms against his eyes until colors bloomed in the darkness.

He wanted to disbelieve it. Wanted to find the flaws in the argument, the gaps in the evidence, the proof that this was MNA propaganda designed to undermine Pale City morale. But the book was not MNA. It had been written by a Pale City scholar, a man who had spent his life in the archives before the Doctrine Keepers had been given authority over historical truth. The man had been executed for sedition two years after publication. His book had been burned. This copy, smuggled through networks Elias was only beginning to understand, was one of perhaps a dozen that still existed.

Everything he had been taught was a lie.

Not a misunderstanding. Not a difference of interpretation. A deliberate, systematic, multigenerational lie designed to justify crimes that were still being committed in its name.

Elias thought of his father, who had served in the Border Guard for thirty years. Who had told stories of MNA raiders and terrorist cells and the constant threat that lurked beyond the walls. Who had given Elias a compass on his sixteenth birthday and said, "Always know which way home is."

Had his father known? Had he killed people believing he

was defending his family from monsters, never understanding that his own leaders had invented those monsters to keep him afraid?

The chemical lamp flickered and dimmed further. Elias did not move to replace it. The darkness felt appropriate.

* * *

Footsteps in the corridor outside.

Elias was on his feet before he consciously registered the sound, the book hidden beneath his blanket, his body pressed into the shadow between two stacks of salvage. Three weeks of hiding had taught him reflexes he had never needed in his old life. Three weeks of listening for the boots that would mean discovery, the voices that would mean interrogation, the silence that would mean he had run out of time.

A knock. Three short, two long, one short. The pattern that meant safe.

He exhaled and moved to the door, sliding back the bolt with hands that were not quite steady. The woman who entered was small and gray-haired, her face lined with the kind of exhaustion that sleep could not cure. She wore the coveralls of a recycling worker, stained with rust and chemical residue, and she carried a cloth bag that smelled of bread.

"Mira," Elias said. "Is there news?"

She set the bag on his makeshift table and did not answer immediately. That hesitation told him more than words could have. He had learned to read the network's silences. They were never good.

"The purges are accelerating," she finally said. "Drax has been given emergency authority over internal security. Anyone connected to the Cultural Ministry is being questioned. Your name has been on the broadcasts."

"I know." He had seen it through a crack in the wall, watching a public screen in the alley outside. His official portrait, the one taken for his diplomatic credentials, displayed beside the word TRAITOR in letters designed to evoke fear and disgust. The commentary had called him a MNA agent, a sleeper operative who had infiltrated the cultural exchange program to steal secrets and sow discord. They had invented a history for him, complete with fabricated evidence and testimonies from colleagues he had never met.

Julienne Drax's work. He recognized her style. She did not simply destroy enemies; she rewrote them. By the time she was finished, the person you had been no longer existed. Only the monster she had created in your place.

"There's more," Mira said. She sat heavily on the only chair, a salvaged thing with one leg shorter than the others. "Your family home was raided this morning. Your mother is being held for questioning. Your father's military record is being reviewed for evidence of disloyalty."

Elias felt the words land like blows to the chest. He had known this was possible. Had known that his choices would not affect only himself. But knowing and feeling were different continents, and the distance between them was measured in grief.

"They don't know anything," he said. "I never told them. I never even hinted."

"That won't matter to Drax. Guilt by association doesn't require actual guilt. It only requires a useful narrative." Mira's voice was not unkind, but it held no comfort. She had seen too much to offer false hope. "Your father's reputation is already being dismantled. The broadcasts are calling him a sympathizer. His service record is being reinterpreted. Every commendation is now evidence of something sinister."

Thirty years. Thirty years of waking before dawn to patrol borders his leaders had told him were sacred. Thirty years of missing birthdays and holidays and the small moments that made a family. Thirty years of believing he was protecting his people from an enemy that had never wanted to be an enemy at all.

And now, because his son had discovered the truth, all of it would be erased. Rewritten. Turned into another weapon in the arsenal of lies.

"Is there anything I can do?" Elias asked. The question felt pathetic even as he spoke it. He was hiding in a storage room, dependent on strangers for food and information, unable to show his face on any street in the city where he had been born. He could do nothing for his parents. He could barely do anything for himself.

"You can survive," Mira said. "That's what they don't want. Every day you stay free is a day their narrative has a hole in it. Every day you're alive to tell what you know is a day the truth exists somewhere outside their control."

"That's not enough."

"It's what we have." She reached into her bag and withdrew a folded paper. "There's something else. The extraction."

Elias's heart stuttered. The extraction. The mission he had made possible with his intelligence about the detention facility, the patrol schedules, the access codes. The mission that was supposed to bring MNA prisoners home and prove that the underground could hurt the Pale Cities where it mattered.

"It's happening tonight," Mira said. "They're already moving. If everything goes according to plan, the prisoners will be across the border by dawn."

"If."

"If." She unfolded the paper. It was a map, hand-drawn, showing the facility and its surroundings. Red marks indicated the team's approach routes. Blue marks indicated extraction points. "We won't know if it worked until morning. Maybe longer. Communications are monitored more heavily than ever."

Elias studied the map. Saw his own intelligence reflected in the red lines, the careful approach through the industrial ruins, the entry points he had identified from classified briefings. Lives were being risked on information he had provided. People he would never meet were trusting him with their survival.

"What if I was wrong?" he said. The fear had been growing in him for days, a cold pressure in his chest that would not ease. "What if the information was outdated? What if they changed the protocols after I defected?"

"Then people will die." Mira's voice was flat. Matter-of-fact. "That's the nature of what we do. We act on imperfect information because perfect information doesn't exist. We make choices that might be wrong because not choosing is also a choice, and usually a worse one."

"That's not comforting."

"It's not meant to be. Comfort is a luxury we lost the moment we started asking questions." She stood, leaving the bread and the map on the table. "Eat something. Try to sleep. I'll bring word when we have it."

She was at the door when Elias spoke again. "Mira. Why do you do this?"

She paused, her hand on the bolt. "Do what?"

"Risk everything. Hide people like me. Fight a system that will crush you if it finds you." He gestured at the cramped, dim room, at the recycling facility humming beyond the walls, at the city of ten million people who would call her a traitor if they knew her name. "Why?"

Mira was quiet for a long moment. When she answered, her voice was softer than he had ever heard it.

"I had a son," she said. "He asked a question in school. About the history. About whether the official version was true." A pause. A breath. "He was fourteen. They took him for re-education. He came back different. Quiet. Empty. He stopped asking questions. He stopped asking anything. Two years later, he walked into the river and didn't walk out."

Elias did not know what to say. There was nothing to say.

"I do this," Mira continued, "because the system that killed my son is still killing other people's sons. And daughters. And parents. And anyone else who notices that the emperor has no clothes." She opened the door. "I do this because someone has to. And because I'm already dead inside, so I have nothing left to lose."

She was gone before he could respond. The bolt slid home. The footsteps faded. And Elias was alone again with the silence and the dying lamp and the weight of a truth he had not asked to carry.

* * *

He could not sleep.

The bread sat untouched on the table. The map lay open beside it, its red and blue lines becoming a landscape he could navigate with closed eyes. Elias paced the narrow space between the salvage stacks, counting steps, trying to exhaust a body that refused to be exhausted.

Somewhere beyond these walls, people were fighting. Somewhere in the darkness of the Frontier, MNA operatives were approaching the detention facility with his intelligence as their guide. Somewhere, a woman named Renna and a man named Kele were waiting to be rescued or waiting to be used as bait or already dead in cells he had helped the rescuers find.

He pulled his father's compass from his pocket. The needle pointed east, as it always did. Toward the apartment where he had grown up. Toward the room where his mother was now being questioned about a son she did not understand. Toward a father whose life's work was being dismantled because Elias had decided the truth mattered more than peace.

Had it been worth it?

The question haunted him. He had believed, when he first made contact with the underground, that exposing the lies would change something. That people would wake up, would see what their leaders had done, would demand a different future. He had imagined a revolution of conscience, a collective turning away from the propaganda that had poisoned three generations.

Instead, there were purges. Arrests. His face on wanted posters. His family's destruction. And a city that seemed, if anything, more committed to its lies than ever.

Through the thin walls, the Signal Mesh droned on. A night broadcast, the kind designed to reach insomniacs and shift workers, its tone softer than the daytime programming but no less insidious. The voice was warm, paternal, speaking of the threats beyond the borders and the vigilance required to meet them.

"...MNA aggression continues to destabilize the region. Citizens are reminded to report any suspicious activity to their local security office. Together, we will preserve the peace our ancestors died to build..."

Elias wanted to scream. Wanted to broadcast his own voice over those frequencies, to tell everyone listening that the peace was built on corpses and the ancestors had been the aggressors. But the Signal Mesh was controlled by the Doctrine Keepers, and the Doctrine Keepers answered to Julienne Drax, and Drax would sooner burn the city than let a contrary word reach its inhabitants.

He sat on his pallet and held the compass in both hands. The metal was warm from his pocket, the glass scratched from years of use. His father had carried it through his entire career, had told Elias it was the only thing that had never lied to him.

But the compass didn't point toward truth. It only pointed toward magnetic north. It only told you which direction you were facing, not whether the direction was right.

Elias thought about the extraction team, moving through the darkness at this very moment. He thought about the faces in the detention facility, the prisoners who might be free by morning or might be dead by morning depending on whether his information was accurate. He thought about Mira's son, walking into the river because the questions in his head had nowhere else to go.

He thought about what it meant to betray a country that had already betrayed you.

The lamp finally died. The room plunged into darkness, broken only by the faint glow seeping through cracks in the walls, the ambient light of a city that never truly slept. Elias sat in that darkness and listened to the Signal Mesh murmur its endless reassurances and tried to believe that what he had done would matter.

Somewhere, the extraction was underway.

Somewhere, people were risking their lives because of him.

All he could do was wait. And hope. And try not to think about all the ways hope could be betrayed.

* * *

Dawn came gray and uncertain, filtering through the gaps in the walls like something ashamed to be seen.

Elias had not slept. He had spent the night alternating between the book and the map, between forbidden history and present-tense danger. His eyes burned. His thoughts moved slowly, as though wading through thick water.

He was trying to focus on a passage about pre-contact trade networks when the knock came. Not the safe pattern. A different one. Urgent. Incomplete.

His body moved before his mind caught up, pressing into shadow, hand reaching for the small knife that was his only weapon. The bolt rattled. The door opened.

Mira. Her face was pale, her movements jerky with the specific energy of disaster.

"The safe houses," she said. "They know about the safe houses."

Elias felt the floor shift beneath him. "How?"

"We don't know. Someone talked. Someone was followed. It doesn't matter. What matters is they're moving. Security forces hit the eastern network an hour ago. Twelve arrests. Maybe more."

"The extraction?"

"No word. Communications are down across the board. Either they made it or they didn't. We won't know until someone gets a message through." She grabbed his arm, her grip stronger than her small frame suggested. "You have to move. Now. This location could be compromised within hours."

Elias looked at the room that had been his prison and his sanctuary for nine days. The pallet. The salvage stacks. The dying lamp he had not replaced. The book of forbidden history, still sitting on the table where anyone who searched the room would find it.

"Where?" he asked.

"There's one more location. Further into the industrial sector. It's not comfortable, but it's the most isolated we have." She released his arm and handed him a folded paper. "Memorize this route. Burn the paper. Leave nothing behind."

He took the paper. Looked at Mira's exhausted face, at the fear she was trying to hide behind efficiency. "Twelve arrests. Were any of them people I knew?"

"Does it matter?"

"Yes."

She was silent for a moment. Then: "Varro. The one who brought you in. He was one of the first taken."

Varro. A middle-aged archivist with kind eyes and a habit of humming old songs while he worked. He had found Elias in the chaos after the summit, had recognized the look of a man whose world was collapsing, had offered shelter without asking for anything in return.

"He won't talk," Mira said. "He knows what's at stake."

"Everyone talks eventually." Elias had read the intelligence reports about Pale City interrogation methods. He knew what Drax's people could do to a person's mind, the techniques that left no physical marks but dismantled identity piece by piece. "It's just a matter of time."

"Then we use the time we have." Mira moved toward the door. "Five minutes. Gather what you need. Destroy what you can't carry."

She was gone. Elias stood in the gray dawn light and tried to make his mind work. Gather. Destroy. Move. Simple instructions for someone whose life had become a series of desperate improvisations.

He picked up the book first. The forbidden history. His evidence that everything he had been taught was a lie. He could not carry it. It was too large, too recognizable. If he was stopped and searched, it would be his death sentence.

But he could not destroy it either. This copy might be one of the last in existence. To burn it would be to participate in the same erasure the Doctrine Keepers practiced.

He hid it instead. Found a gap between two salvage bales where the metal had warped, creating a cavity just large enough. Wrapped the book in his spare shirt to protect it from moisture. Wedged it into the darkness where it might wait for years, for decades, for someone who needed to know what it contained.

The compass he kept. His father's compass, pointing east toward a home that was no longer home. It was small enough to hide, and he was not ready to let go of everything.

He memorized the route on Mira's paper, then burned it in the chemical lamp's dying ember. Watched the ashes curl and scatter.

And then he left the storage room behind the recycling facility and stepped into the uncertain gray of a morning that promised nothing but survival, if he was lucky, and discovery, if he was not.

The Signal Mesh was broadcasting news of MNA terrorism. The facility that had held MNA prisoners had been attacked in the night. Casualties reported. Investigations underway. Citizens urged to remain vigilant.

Elias listened to the broadcast and tried to parse the propaganda. An attack on the facility could mean the extraction had worked. Or it could mean the extraction had failed catastrophically. Or it could mean something else entirely, some truth that the Doctrine Keepers would never allow on the airwaves.

He walked through the industrial sector with his head down and his collar up, one more anonymous figure in a city of millions. Around him, workers shuffled toward morning shifts, their faces blank with the particular exhaustion of people who had stopped expecting anything better. The sky above was the color of old metal, and the air tasted of smoke and chemistry.

Somewhere beyond the walls, the MNA was waking to whatever the night had brought them.

Somewhere, Aiyana Waketah and her team were alive or dead.

And somewhere, in the depths of the Doctrine Keepers' archives, Julienne Drax was already crafting the story that would be told about this night, reshaping reality to fit the narrative she required.

Elias found the new safe house. A basement beneath a warehouse, smaller and darker than the last. He descended the stairs and sat in the corner and waited for news that might never come.

The compass needle pointed east.

But east was not the only direction anymore.

Elias looked at the compass for a long moment. Then he closed his eyes and let himself imagine, for just a moment, what lay to the west. Beyond the walls. Beyond the propaganda. Beyond everything he had been taught to fear.

The Many Nations Alliance.

The enemy that had never wanted to be an enemy.

The truth that was worth dying for, if it came to that.

Elias opened his eyes.
And began to plan.

3

The Holding Cells

The eastern wing smelled of fear.

Not metaphorically. Fear had a chemistry, a signature of sweat and stress hormones and the particular exhalation of people who had lived too long without hope. Aiyana tasted it the moment she stepped through the ruined doorway, a thickness in the air that her sky-suit's filters could not quite scrub clean.

The corridor ahead was longer than the one she had left behind. The lighting here was different: not the flat, shadowless illumination of the western detention block, but something harsher, more clinical. Observation lights, she realized. The kind designed to leave no corner unwatched. The kind used in places where watching was the point.

The alarms screamed around her, a sound designed to disorient, to make thought difficult. She pushed through it the way she had been trained, letting the noise become background, focusing on what mattered. Sitala's awareness flickered at the edge of her consciousness, the eagle circling above the facility in growing agitation. Through their bond,

Aiyana sensed movement: guards converging from multiple directions, vehicles starting in the motor pool, the coordinated response of a military installation waking to threat.

She had minutes. Maybe less.

The first cell she passed was empty, its door standing open. The second held a man curled in the corner, hands over his ears, rocking. He did not look up as she passed. The third, the fourth, the fifth: more prisoners, more Pale City faces, more evidence of what this place truly was.

This was not just a detention facility. This was an interrogation center. The kind of place where people were brought not to be held but to be broken.

Renna had said they were asking Kele about the Bioweb. About how it worked. The implications of that made Aiyana's stomach turn. The Nullwave had damaged MNA technology in ways that were still being assessed. If the Quiet Choir was trying to understand Bioweb architecture, if they were extracting that knowledge from prisoners...

She moved faster.

A junction ahead. Left led deeper into the facility, toward what looked like administrative offices. Right curved toward a reinforced section, additional security doors, the architecture of maximum containment. That was where they would keep the most valuable prisoners. That was where Kele would be.

Aiyana turned right and nearly collided with a guard.

He was young, barely older than her, his face still soft with the remnants of adolescence. He wore the gray uniform of facility security, and his hand was moving toward the weapon at his hip, but too slowly. Too surprised. He had not expected to find an intruder here, in the heart of the most secure section.

Aiyana's sky-suit responded before she consciously commanded it. The organic circuitry pulsed, channeling harmonic energy through her palm. She pressed her hand against his chest and released the charge.

The guard's eyes went wide. His body stiffened, then went limp. She caught him as he fell, lowered him to the floor as gently as she could manage. He was breathing. He would wake in an hour with a headache and confused memories. It was more mercy than the Pale Cities showed their prisoners.

She took his access card. The security doors would need more than Elias's codes.

The reinforced section opened onto a short hallway with only three doors. Maximum containment. The prisoners here were either the most dangerous or the most valuable. Given what Renna had said, Aiyana suspected Kele was the latter.

The first door: empty cell, recently vacated. Signs of habitation still visible, a thin mattress indented by the shape of a body, marks on the wall that might have been counting days.

The second door: a woman, MNA by her features, but Aiyana did not recognize her. The woman was sitting on her cot, staring at nothing, her lips moving in a conversation with someone who was not there. Whatever had been done to her in this place had left her somewhere beyond reach.

Aiyana hesitated. She could not carry two people. She could barely guarantee she could get Kele out. But leaving this woman here, leaving her to whatever fate awaited...

"I'll come back," she said through the door, knowing the woman probably could not hear her, knowing she might be lying. "I'll come back for you."

The third door.

The access card worked. The lock disengaged with a heavy thunk. The door swung open.

Kele was on the floor.

He lay curled on his side, facing the wall, his body drawn tight as if trying to make itself as small as possible. He wore the same institutional gray as the other prisoners, but his was stained, torn at the shoulder, marked with evidence of rough handling. His hair, which Aiyana remembered as carefully braided, had been shorn close to the scalp. His hands, visible where they pressed against his chest, were trembling.

"Kele." She kept her voice soft, aware that sudden sounds might trigger a response she could not predict. "Kele, it's Aiyana. I'm here to take you home."

He did not move. Did not acknowledge her presence. His trembling continued, a constant vibration that seemed to have become part of his body's baseline state.

She crossed the cell and knelt beside him. Up close, she could see more: the bruises on his neck, faded to yellow-green, weeks old. The rawness around his wrists where restraints had worn through skin. The way his breathing came in short, shallow bursts, the rhythm of someone who had learned that deep breaths could be dangerous.

"Kele." She touched his shoulder, and he flinched so violently that she jerked her hand back. "It's okay. I'm MNA. I'm a Sky Guardian. We're getting you out."

Slowly, with the hesitance of an animal expecting a trap, he turned his head. His eyes found her face. For a long moment, there was nothing there, just the blank watchfulness of someone who had stopped believing in rescue.

Then something shifted. Recognition, perhaps. Or hope, that most dangerous of emotions.

"Aiyana." His voice was a ruin, scraped raw by screaming or disuse or both. "You're... you're real?"

"I'm real. Can you stand?"

He tried. She watched the effort it cost him, the way his muscles refused to cooperate, the way his body had forgotten how to trust its own commands. She helped him up, took his weight against her shoulder, felt how much of him had been worn away in the weeks since his capture.

"They asked questions," he said as she guided him toward the door. "About the Bioweb. About the resonance frequencies. About how it connects to living things." A shudder ran through him. "I tried not to answer. I tried. But they have... they have ways."

"You don't have to explain."

"I have to explain." His grip on her arm tightened, sudden and fierce. "I have to tell someone. They made me see things. Hear things. I don't know what was real anymore. I don't know what I told them."

Aiyana felt cold spread through her chest. Interrogation was one thing. But what Kele was describing sounded like something else. Something that went beyond extracting information into something that dismantled the mind itself.

"Later," she said. "You can tell me everything later. Right now, we need to move."

They made it three steps into the corridor before the shooting started.

* * *

The projectiles were not bullets.

Aiyana registered that in the fraction of a second before she pulled Kele down, throwing them both behind the minimal cover of a doorframe. The weapons the Pale Cities used against MNA targets were designed to disrupt harmonic technology. Energy pulses that interfered with the Bioweb frequencies, that could shut down a sky-suit, that could sever the bond between a Guardian and their animal companion.

She had trained against these weapons. She knew their limitations. They were powerful at close range but lost coherence over distance. They required a direct hit to cause significant damage. And they could be countered, briefly, by the defensive frequencies her sky-suit was designed to generate.

She activated the countermeasures and felt the suit respond, a shimmer of protective resonance spreading across her skin. It would not last long. The power required was enormous, draining reserves faster than they could regenerate.

Three guards at the end of the corridor. Gray uniforms. Angular weapons that hummed with contained energy. They advanced in formation, covering each other, professional and coordinated.

"Stay down," she told Kele.

She did not wait for his response. Her sky-suit's flight membranes extended from her forearms as she launched herself forward, not flying, not in this enclosed space, but using the membranes to catch air, to change direction mid-stride, to make herself unpredictable.

The first guard fired. Aiyana twisted, the pulse passing close enough that she felt the hairs on her arm stand up from the electromagnetic discharge. She closed the distance and struck him in the throat with the edge of her hand, pulling the blow at the last instant so it incapacitated rather than killed.

The second guard adjusted aim. Aiyana grabbed the first guard's body as it fell, using it as a shield. The pulse hit the unconscious man, and she felt the impact through his mass, a wrongness that vibrated through her bones.

She threw the body at the second guard, followed it with her own momentum. They went down together, a tangle of limbs and weapons. Her sky-suit pulsed again, channeling harmonic energy through her palm, and the guard went limp beneath her.

The third guard was smarter than his colleagues. He had fallen back, was calling for reinforcements on his communicator, was buying time for forces Aiyana could not fight alone.

She sprinted toward him. He fired. The pulse caught her shoulder, and for a terrifying instant, her sky-suit flickered, its organic systems struggling against the disruption. She stumbled, felt the bond with Sitala waver like a candle flame in wind.

Then her suit stabilized. She reached the guard. Her fist connected with his jaw. He dropped.

Aiyana stood in the corridor, breathing hard, her shoulder burning where the pulse had hit. Around her, three guards lay unconscious. Through her recovering bond, she felt Sitala's relief, the eagle's fear that had spiked when their connection wavered.

I'm all right, she sent. *Watch the approaches. Tell me what's coming.*

The answer came in images rather than words: vehicles mobilizing, guards pouring from the main building, a perimeter being established. The facility was going into full lockdown. Every exit would be covered within minutes.

"Kele." She ran back to the doorway where she had left him. He was huddled against the wall, arms wrapped around himself, eyes wide. The violence had triggered something. She could see it in the way he rocked, in the small sounds he was making, in the disconnection from the present moment. "Kele, I need you to focus. We have to go."

He looked at her but did not seem to see her.

She crouched beside him, took his face in her hands, made him meet her eyes. "Kele. I know you're somewhere else right now. I know what they did put you in a place you can't easily leave. But I need you here. Just for a little while. Just until we're safe."

Something in her voice reached him. The rocking slowed. His breathing deepened, became more deliberate. When he spoke, his voice was distant but present.

"The roof. There's... there's roof access at the end of the south corridor. I heard the guards talking about it. They use it for observation."

The roof. Aiyana's sky-suit could carry her, could carry them both if she pushed it to the limit. If they could reach open air, Sitala could provide cover, and they could fly over the walls before the guards could bring them down.

It was a terrible plan. It was the only plan she had.

"Can you run?"

"I don't know."

"Then we find out."

She pulled him upright, steadied him, pointed him toward the south corridor. He took a step. Then another. His gait was uneven, his body still fighting itself, but he was moving.

They ran.

* * *

The south corridor was longer than Aiyana had hoped.

They passed more cells, more prisoners who watched with hollow eyes as two figures sprinted past. Aiyana wanted to stop, wanted to free every one of them, wanted to tear this place down brick by brick. But she could not carry everyone. She could barely carry herself and Kele.

The alarms had shifted to a different pattern now, deeper, more insistent. Lockdown alarms. Every door in the facility would be sealing. They had seconds before their path was cut off.

"There." Kele pointed with a shaking hand. A stairwell at the end of the corridor, a metal door already beginning to swing closed on automatic hinges.

Aiyana pushed herself faster, dragging Kele with her. The door was half closed. Three quarters. They would not make it. They would be sealed in this corridor, trapped, waiting for the guards to come.

She extended her free hand and released everything her sky-suit had left. The harmonic pulse hit the door's mechanism, disrupting the electronics that controlled its closing. The door shuddered, stopped, began to slide open again as the damaged system reset.

They slipped through. The door resumed closing behind them, sealing with a heavy clang.

The stairwell was narrow, utilitarian, designed for maintenance access rather than regular traffic. Aiyana took the steps two at a time, pulling Kele with her, feeling his exhaustion through the way he leaned on her, through the small sounds of pain he could not quite suppress.

One flight. Two. Three. Her own legs burned. Her shoulder throbbed where the pulse had hit. Through her bond, Sitala tracked the guards on the roof, two of them, armed but not yet aware that targets were ascending.

A door at the top. Locked. Aiyana did not slow down. She hit it at full speed, her sky-suit absorbing the impact, channeling the force into the frame. The lock held. The frame did not. The door burst outward, and they spilled onto the roof in a tumble of limbs and cold morning air.

The guards turned. Saw them. Raised weapons.

Sitala hit the first guard from above, talons raking across his face, wings battering his head. The man screamed and fell back, weapon discharging harmlessly into the sky.

Aiyana was already moving toward the second. He was trying to track the eagle and the intruders simultaneously, dividing his attention in a way that left him vulnerable. Her fist connected with his solar plexus. He doubled over. Her knee came up into his face. He went down.

The roof stretched around them, flat and gray, studded with ventilation equipment and observation posts. The sky above was lightening toward dawn, bands of color bleeding through the smog that hung perpetually over Pale City territory. Beyond the walls, Aiyana could see the Frontier, the scarred landscape that separated two worlds.

Home was that direction. Safety was that direction. All she had to do was fly.

"Kele." She pulled him close, wrapping her arms around his chest. "Hold onto me. Don't let go."

"I can't." His voice was barely a whisper. "I can't. It's too high. They'll shoot us down."

"Sitala will cover us. I'll fly low, use the terrain." She tightened her grip. "Trust me."

Through their bond, she felt Sitala's presence, the eagle already climbing, already positioning herself between the escapees and the guards below. Arrows of attention focused on them from the ground. Weapons were being aimed. In seconds, the air would fill with the hum of disruptor fire.

Aiyana's sky-suit spread its membranes. She felt the familiar tension in the organic material, the way it caught the air, the potential energy waiting to be released.

"Waketah." A voice behind her. Amplified. Commanding.

She turned.

Commander Speaks-Low stood at the far edge of the roof, flanked by Pale City soldiers. His hands were bound in front of him. His face was bloodied. And behind him, a woman in gray pressed a weapon to the back of his head.

"You can fly," the woman called. Her voice was calm, almost conversational. "Your companion cannot follow. And if you leave, this one dies."

Aiyana's heart stopped.

Speaks-Low. They had Speaks-Low.

His eyes found hers across the rooftop. In them, she saw pain and determination and something that looked terribly like acceptance.

"Go," he said. The word was quiet, meant only for her, but it carried across the dawn air like a command. "Complete the mission. Go."

The woman pressed the weapon harder against his skull. "Decide now, Waketah. Your commander's life, or the prisoner you came for. You cannot have both."

Kele's arms tightened around her. His breath came in ragged gasps against her neck. He was not capable of making this choice. He was barely capable of standing. It was her burden, her call, her impossible mathematics of survival.

Speaks-Low had led her. Trained her. Believed in her when she had not believed in herself. He was the reason she was a Guardian at all.

Kele was broken, might never fully recover, but carried secrets in his damaged mind that the Quiet Choir wanted desperately to extract.

"Go," Speaks-Low said again. Louder this time. An order.

Aiyana looked at her commander. Looked at the woman who held his life in her hands. Looked at the dawn breaking over a world that had no room for mercy.

She jumped.

The sky-suit's membranes caught the air. Kele screamed against her shoulder. Below them, disruptor fire lit the morning, pulses of energy cutting through the space they had occupied a moment before.

Sitala dove between them and their pursuers, a golden blur of feathers and fury, drawing fire, creating chaos. Aiyana flew low, using the facility's structures as cover, skimming over walls and fences and the gray expanse of the Frontier beyond.

She did not look back.

She could not bear to look back.

Speaks-Low's face stayed with her anyway, that expression of acceptance, that quiet command that was also a farewell. She had obeyed him. She had left him. She had done what the mission required.

The border approached, an invisible line that separated death from survival. Her suit's power reserves were nearly depleted. Kele had stopped screaming and gone limp against her, his consciousness finally surrendering to the trauma of rescue.

They crossed the line. They were in MNA territory. They were safe.

Aiyana found a place to land, a clearing in a forest that was green and alive, a stark contrast to the dead lands they had left behind. She set Kele down gently, checked his pulse, confirmed he was still breathing.

Then she sat beside him in the morning light, Sitala settling on her shoulder with a weight that felt like comfort and accusation in equal measure.

She thought about Renna, hopefully safe with Catches-The-Wind by now.

She thought about Speaks-Low, certainly a prisoner, certainly facing interrogation, certainly blaming himself for the failure of a mission that had been compromised from the start.

She thought about Elias Harren, whose codes had sprung the trap, whose intelligence had led them into this disaster.

And she thought about what came next. The debriefing. The questions. The moment when she would have to explain why Commander Speaks-Low was not with her, why she had left him behind, why she had followed his final order even though following it had broken something inside her that might never heal.

The sun rose over the mountains. The Bioweb hummed around her, a song of connection and life, a reminder of everything her people had built and everything the Pale Cities wanted to destroy.

Aiyana closed her eyes and let herself feel all of it: the grief, the guilt, the fury, the exhaustion.

Then she opened her eyes and began the work of survival.

The mission was not over. It had only changed shape.

And somewhere behind her, in a facility that had been designed to break human beings, a man who had spent his life serving the Many Nations Alliance was paying the price for her escape.

4

The Cost

Wakana Station rose from the forest like something that had grown rather than been built.

The towers were shaped by wind and time, their surfaces textured with the whorls of living wood that had been guided into form over generations. Bridges of woven fiber connected platforms at different heights, swaying gently in the mountain breeze. Birds nested in alcoves that had been designed for them, their songs joining the deeper hum of the Bioweb that pulsed through every structure, every root, every breath of air.

Aiyana had always loved returning here. The station had been her home during training, the place where she had learned to fly, to fight, to bond with Sitala. Every path held memories. Every tower had witnessed some small triumph or failure that had shaped who she became.

Today, it felt like a place she no longer deserved.

The medical team had met them at the border crossing, alerted by the emergency beacon Aiyana had finally activated once they were safely in MNA territory. They had taken Kele immediately, lifting his unconscious form onto a stretcher woven from living vines that would monitor his vitals and begin the slow work of healing. Renna had arrived an hour later with Catches-The-Wind, exhausted but intact, her eyes finding Aiyana's across the clearing with a look that held too many questions.

Talon and River-Runs-Deep had not returned.

No one had said the words yet. No one had confirmed what the silence meant. But Aiyana had seen enough combat to understand the mathematics of absence. Two Guardians sent with Speaks-Low's team. Two Guardians unaccounted for. Two more names that would be added to the memorial wall if the worst was true.

She stood now on an observation platform high above the station's central clearing, watching the sun climb toward noon. Sitala perched beside her, the eagle's injured wing held carefully against her body. The wound was not serious, a graze from a disruptor pulse that had singed feathers and bruised the delicate structures beneath, but it would take days to heal properly. Days during which Sitala could not fly, during which their bond would feel the strain of her companion's discomfort.

Aiyana had refused treatment for her own injuries. The burn on her shoulder, the bruises from the fighting, the exhaustion that made her bones feel hollow. She did not deserve to be healed while Speaks-Low was still in enemy hands.

"You should rest."

The voice came from behind her. She did not turn. She had felt his approach through the Bioweb, the distinctive pattern of his presence that she had known since childhood.

"Elder Grayfeather."

Chogan moved to stand beside her at the railing. He was older than when she had last seen him, or perhaps he simply looked older, the weight of recent weeks visible in the lines of his face and the gray threading through his hair. He wore the simple robes of a diplomat, not the formal attire of a Council member, and she wondered if that was intentional. A signal that this conversation was personal rather than official.

"I spoke with Catches-The-Wind," he said. "He told me what happened. What you did."

"I left him." The words tasted like ash. "Speaks-Low ordered me to go, and I left him."

"You followed a direct command from your superior officer in a combat situation. You extracted the primary objective. You survived to report." Chogan's voice was measured, careful. "By any military standard, you did exactly what you should have done."

"Military standards." She turned to face him, and something in her expression made him take a half-step back. "He trained me. For three years, he trained me. He taught me how to fly, how to fight, how to think. And when they had a weapon to his head, I flew away."

"What would you have done differently?"

The question stopped her. She had been asking herself the same thing for hours, replaying the moment on the rooftop, searching for the choice she had not made, the path she had not seen.

"I don't know," she admitted. "Surrendered. Fought. Died trying to save him."

"And Kele? The man you were sent to rescue? The man who carries information the Quiet Choir desperately wants?" Chogan shook his head slowly. "You would have given them two prisoners instead of one. You would have given them everything they wanted."

"I know." Her voice cracked. "I know all of that. It doesn't help."

Chogan was quiet for a long moment. When he spoke again, his voice had softened.

"Speaks-Low and I have known each other for thirty years. We trained together, served together, disagreed about almost everything that matters." A ghost of a smile crossed his face. "He is the most stubborn man I have ever met. And he is my friend."

Aiyana looked at him, seeing for the first time the grief he was carrying beneath the diplomatic composure.

"When he ordered you to go," Chogan continued, "he was not sacrificing himself for the mission. He was sacrificing himself for you. Because he believed you were worth saving. Because he saw something in you that he wanted to protect." He met her eyes. "Do not dishonor that choice by destroying yourself with guilt."

"How do I honor it?"

"By surviving. By becoming what he believed you could be. By making sure his sacrifice means something." Chogan turned back to the view, the endless green of the forest, the distant peaks still touched with snow. "And by helping us bring him home."

Aiyana felt something shift in her chest. Not relief, not forgiveness, but something adjacent to both. A direction. A purpose.

"How?"

"That is what we need to discuss. But first, you need to understand what we are facing." Chogan's expression hardened. "The mission was compromised from the beginning. The codes your contact provided were genuine, but they were also known to Pale City intelligence. Someone fed them to your source knowing they would be passed along. The entire extraction was a trap designed to capture MNA operatives."

"Elias." The name felt strange in her mouth, foreign and familiar at once. "He betrayed us?"

"We do not believe so. Our assessment is that he was given false information by people who suspected his loyalties. They used him as a channel to reach us." Chogan paused. "He is still sending messages. Still trying to help. He does not know that his intelligence nearly got you all killed."

"Should someone tell him?"

"That is a complicated question. If we tell him the truth, we risk breaking a valuable asset at a time when we need every advantage. If we do not tell him, we risk him sending more compromised information." Chogan sighed. "There are no good options. Only less terrible ones."

Aiyana thought about the young man in the intelligence photographs, the earnest eyes, the apparent sincerity. She had wondered if she could trust him. Now she wondered if trust was even the right framework. He had not betrayed them. He had been used. The distinction mattered, even if the outcome was the same.

"There's more," Chogan said. "The network that helped Elias is collapsing. The Pale Cities are conducting purges. Safe houses have been raided. People have been arrested. The underground that has been feeding us information for years is being systematically destroyed."

"Because of us? Because of the extraction?"

"Partially. The raid gave them justification. But this was already in motion. Julienne Drax has been consolidating power since the summit. She is eliminating anyone who might question the official narrative." He shook his head. "We are watching a society consume itself from within. It would be encouraging if it were not so dangerous."

Sitala stirred beside Aiyana, the eagle's attention shifting toward the eastern sky. Through their bond, Aiyana felt a whisper of warning, a sense that something was approaching.

"Someone is coming," she said.

Chogan nodded. He had been expecting this. "A messenger. From the border network. There is news about Elias."

* * *

The messenger was young, barely more than a teenager, wearing the practical clothing of a border runner.

She found them on the observation platform and delivered her report with the clipped efficiency of someone who had memorized words meant for other ears. The safe house network in Nova-Providence was evacuating. Elias Harren had been moved twice in the past day. He was requesting extraction.

"He wants to come here," Aiyana said when the messenger had finished. "Now. After everything that just happened."

"He believes he is running out of time," Chogan said. "The purges are closing around him. If he stays, he will be captured. If he is captured, he will be made to reveal everything he knows about the underground, about us, about our methods and contacts."

"So we extract him to protect ourselves."

"Partially. But also because he has value beyond what he has already given us. He was a cultural envoy. He had access to archives, to official histories, to the machinery of Pale City propaganda. What he knows could help us understand how they think, how they plan, how they might be countered."

Chogan met her eyes. "And because leaving him to die when he has risked everything to help us would be a betrayal of who we claim to be."

Aiyana thought about betrayal. About the codes that had been compromised. About Speaks-Low in a cell somewhere, facing the same interrogation methods that had broken Kele. About the terrible arithmetic of war that made human beings into variables in equations of survival.

"When?" she asked.

"That is the complication." Chogan's expression tightened. "The summit negotiations resume in four days. Both sides have agreed to proceed despite the incident at the detention facility. The Pale Cities are calling it a terrorist attack. We are calling it a rescue operation. Neither narrative will survive contact with the other, but diplomacy requires the pretense of communication."

"You want to extract Elias during the summit."

"It is our best opportunity. Pale City attention will be focused on the negotiations. Security resources will be allocated to protecting their delegation rather than hunting fugitives. And if the extraction goes wrong..." He paused. "If it goes wrong during the summit, we have diplomatic cover. We can claim it was a rogue operation, disavow involvement, maintain the pretense of good faith."

"While negotiating for Speaks-Low's release."

"Yes."

Aiyana saw it then, the shape of what Chogan was proposing. A public face of diplomacy, seeking the return of a captured commander through official channels. A hidden operation, extracting an asset under cover of the negotiations. Two games being played simultaneously, each providing cover for the other.

It was the kind of thinking Speaks-Low would have admired. Layered. Strategic. Ruthlessly practical.

"You want me to be part of this," she said. It was not a question.

"I want you to lead it." Chogan held up a hand before she could respond. "You know the terrain. You have experience with the detention facility's security. You have met Renna, who knows the underground network. And you have more motivation than anyone else to see this through."

"Because of Speaks-Low."

"Because of Speaks-Low. Because of what the Pale Cities did to Kele. Because of what they will do to Elias if we leave him behind." Chogan's voice hardened. "And because I need someone who understands that this is not just about one man. This is about whether we can operate inside their territory, whether we can protect our people, whether we can fight this war on terms that do not destroy who we are."

The weight of it settled on Aiyana's shoulders. Leadership. Responsibility. The chance to make right what had gone wrong, or the chance to fail again on a larger scale.

"I need to think," she said.

"Of course. But not for long. The summit begins in four days. We need to be ready." Chogan turned to leave, then paused. "Visit Renna before you decide. She has things to tell you. Things that may affect your choice."

He descended the platform's spiral stairs, leaving Aiyana alone with Sitala and the endless sky.

* * *

The medical wing was built into the oldest tree in Wakana Station, a grandmother oak that had been growing before the first human settlements existed on this continent.

Aiyana climbed the winding stairs carved into its trunk, passing levels dedicated to different kinds of healing. Physical trauma on the lower floors, where the Bioweb connection was strongest. Psychological care higher up, where the light filtered soft and green through leaves that had witnessed centuries of human suffering and recovery.

Renna's room was near the top. The door was open, and Aiyana paused in the threshold, uncertain whether to enter.

The woman inside was not the same woman she had found in the detention cell. Renna had been bathed, fed, dressed in soft MNA clothing that draped loosely over her too-thin frame. Her hair had been washed and combed, revealing the places where it had been roughly cut. She sat in a chair by the window, staring out at the forest with an expression Aiyana could not read.

"You came," Renna said without turning. "I wondered if you would."

"Chogan said you wanted to speak with me."

"Chogan says a lot of things. Most of them are even true." Now Renna turned, and Aiyana saw the damage that clean clothes and medical care could not hide. The hollows under her eyes. The way her hands never quite stopped moving. The flinch at sudden sounds that came even here, in the safest place the MNA could provide. "Close the door. What I have to tell you is not for general ears."

Aiyana entered and closed the door behind her. The room was small but comfortable, filled with the soft ambient light of bioluminescent panels and the gentle hum of the healing frequencies the tree provided.

"They kept me in isolation for the first week," Renna said.

"Standard procedure. Break the prisoner down before beginning interrogation. But they talked to each other, and they did not know I could hear through the walls." She paused, her hands twisting in her lap. "The codes. The ones your contact provided. They were not compromised by accident."

"Chogan said the same thing. They used Elias as a channel."

"That is true. But it is not the whole truth." Renna met her eyes, and there was something fierce in her gaze, something that had survived everything the Pale Cities had done to her. "The codes came from inside the MNA, Aiyana. Someone in our intelligence network provided them to the underground, knowing they would reach Elias, knowing he would pass them to us."

The words took a moment to register. When they did, Aiyana felt the floor shift beneath her.

"You are saying we have a traitor."

"I am saying we have something worse than a traitor. We have someone who wanted the extraction to fail. Someone who wanted our operatives captured. Someone who is feeding information to the Quiet Choir and using our own networks to do it." Renna's voice was steady, but her hands betrayed her, clenching and unclenching in rhythms of distress. "The guards talked about it. They were expecting us. They knew when we would come, how we would approach, how many we would be. That level of detail does not come from intercepted communications. It comes from someone who helped plan the mission."

Aiyana's mind raced through the implications. If Renna was right, if there was a traitor in MNA intelligence, then no operation was safe. Every plan they made could be anticipated. Every advantage they thought they had could be turned against them.

"Have you told Chogan?"

"I have told him what I know. He is being careful about what he believes and whom he tells." Renna's lips twisted into something that was not quite a smile. "The problem with discovering a traitor is that you do not know how deep the betrayal goes. Chogan trusts you. I am not sure I do. But you saved my life, so I am giving you the same information I gave him."

"Why?"

"Because you are being asked to lead another operation. Because if there is a traitor, they will try to compromise that operation too. And because..." Renna looked away, toward the window, toward the forest that represented everything the Pale Cities had tried to take from her. "Because Speaks-Low did not deserve what happened to him. Neither did Kele. Neither did Talon or River-Runs-Deep. Someone set us up to fail, Aiyana. Someone in our own ranks. And if you are going back into Pale City territory, you need to know that you might be walking into another trap."

Aiyana stood in silence, processing the weight of what she had learned. A traitor. A second mission already compromised before it began. The possibility that Speaks-Low's capture had not been an accident of war but a deliberate sacrifice by someone he trusted.

"Thank you," she said finally. "For telling me."

Renna nodded once, then turned back to the window. The conversation was over.

Aiyana left the medical wing and descended through the grandmother oak, past healers and patients and the soft sounds of recovery. Her shoulder ached where the disruptor pulse had hit. Her heart ached with something harder to name.

Sitala was waiting for her at the base of the tree, the eagle's golden feathers catching the afternoon light. Through their bond, Aiyana felt her companion's concern, the simple animal love that asked no questions and offered no judgments.

What will you do? Sitala asked in the wordless way of their communication.

Aiyana looked up at the sky, the endless blue interrupted by the living towers of Wakana Station, the birds circling, the clouds drifting toward horizons she could not see.

The Cold War had been abstract before. A political reality, a backdrop to her training, a reason for the work the Guardians did. Now it was personal. Speaks-Low in a cell. Kele broken in a medical ward. A traitor somewhere in the ranks. And Elias Harren, the man whose information had started all of this, waiting to be saved or abandoned.

I will do what I have to, she sent back. *I will find out who betrayed us. I will bring Speaks-Low home. And I will make sure no one else pays for someone else's treachery.*

It was not a plan. It was barely a promise. But it was a direction, and right now, direction was all she had.

She found Chogan in the Council chambers and told him she would lead the extraction.

She did not tell him about Renna's warning. Not yet. Not until she knew whom she could trust.

The summit would begin in four days. The extraction would happen during the negotiations. And somewhere in the machinery of the Many Nations Alliance, a traitor was watching, waiting, preparing to betray them again.

Aiyana intended to find them first.

5

The Assembly Convenes

The Assembly of Renewal met in a chamber designed to inspire awe.

Vaulted ceilings rose forty meters above the polished floor, their surfaces etched with scenes from the Long March: the suffering, the sacrifice, the eventual triumph of the founders. Light entered through narrow windows set high in the walls, falling in precise shafts that illuminated the speaker's podium while leaving the galleries in shadow. The architecture was intentional. Those who spoke here were meant to feel elevated, scrutinized, accountable to history itself.

Rowan Halding stood at that podium now, his hands resting on its cold stone surface, and looked out at the faces of the men and women who governed the Pale Cities. Sixty-three representatives from the seven metropolitan sectors, each elected by processes that the Doctrine Keepers carefully managed to ensure appropriate outcomes. They sat in tiered rows that rose toward the shadowed ceiling, their expressions ranging from eager anticipation to carefully masked concern.

They were waiting for him to speak. They were waiting for

him to make sense of the disaster that had unfolded in the night.

"Colleagues." His voice carried easily in the acoustically perfect chamber, amplified by technology hidden in the ancient-looking stone. "You have heard the reports. In the early hours of this morning, MNA operatives conducted a military assault on the Northern Detention Facility. They breached our defenses, engaged our security forces, and extracted two prisoners being held for crimes against the state."

A murmur rippled through the galleries. Rowan let it build, then fade.

"This was not a rescue operation. It was an act of war. The MNA sent armed soldiers into our sovereign territory, killed three of our citizens, and demonstrated their willingness to use military force against civilian installations." He paused, letting the words settle. "The prisoners they extracted were not innocent victims. They were MNA agents who had been conducting espionage operations inside our borders. Their capture was legal, appropriate, and necessary for our security."

The murmur became voices, representatives leaning toward each other, the carefully maintained order of the chamber beginning to fray. Rowan raised a hand.

"I understand your concern. I share it. But I ask you to consider what this attack reveals about our enemy." He stepped out from behind the podium, moving closer to the representatives, making the address feel more intimate. "The MNA claims to value peace. They claim to seek balance and harmony. Yet when we lawfully detained individuals who had violated our sovereignty, they responded with violence. They killed our people. They destroyed our property. And they did so while their diplomats were still negotiating in supposed good faith."

"What do you propose?" The question came from the third tier, a representative from the industrial sector whose name Rowan could not immediately recall. "Are we to abandon the summit?"

"No." Rowan shook his head firmly. "Abandoning diplomacy would give them exactly what they want. It would allow them to paint us as the aggressors, as unwilling to negotiate, as the obstacle to peace." He returned to the podium, gripping its edges. "We will continue the summit. We will negotiate in good faith. And we will use those negotiations to demand accountability for this outrage."

"How?" Another voice, from the second tier. "What leverage do we have?"

Rowan allowed himself a small smile. "We have something they want very badly. During the assault on our facility, our forces captured one of the MNA operatives. A senior commander. He is currently being held in a secure location, and he possesses information that could be invaluable to our security efforts."

The chamber erupted. Representatives shouting questions, demanding details, some calling for immediate retaliation while others urged caution. Rowan stood at the center of the storm, projecting the calm confidence that had carried him to the highest office in the Pale Cities.

Inside, he felt nothing like calm.

* * *

The private chambers behind the Assembly hall were designed for a different kind of conversation.

Here, the ceilings were lower, the lighting softer, the furniture arranged to encourage intimacy rather than intimidation.

Rowan sat in a leather chair that had belonged to three Prime Councillors before him, a glass of water untouched on the table beside him, and listened to his intelligence chief deliver a report that contradicted nearly everything he had just told the Assembly.

"The facility breach was not a surprise attack," Director Vance said. He was a thin man with colorless eyes and a voice that never rose above a murmur, no matter what horrors he was describing. "We had advance warning. The operation was detected before it began."

"Then why did we not stop it?"

"Because stopping it would have revealed the source of our intelligence." Vance's expression did not change. "The codes the MNA used to access the facility came from us. We provided them through a channel we have been cultivating for months. A channel that leads directly into the heart of the MNA's operations."

Rowan felt his jaw tighten. "You used the facility as bait."

"We used the facility as an opportunity. The MNA sent a team of their best operatives, including a commander with decades of institutional knowledge. We captured him. We also gathered extensive data on their tactics, their technology, their command structure." Vance folded his hands. "The operation was a success by any reasonable measure."

"Three of our people are dead."

"Regrettable. But their sacrifice has given us advantages we could not have obtained through any other means." Vance's colorless eyes met Rowan's. "This is war, Prime Councillor. Not the war of speeches and ceremonies, but the war that happens in shadows. Casualties are inevitable."

Rowan wanted to argue. Wanted to demand an accounting for

decisions made without his knowledge, operations conducted without his approval. But he knew how the machinery of power worked. He had risen through it, had learned its rhythms and requirements. The intelligence services operated with autonomy precisely because their work could not survive the scrutiny of public debate.

"The asset," he said instead. "The channel you mentioned. Is it still viable?"

"We believe so. The MNA does not appear to have identified the source of the compromise. They are attributing the failure to their own contact, a defector named Elias Harren." Vance's lips twitched in something that might have been amusement. "He believes he is helping them. He has no idea that every piece of intelligence he provides has been carefully selected to serve our purposes."

"And the real source? The one inside the MNA?"

"Remains protected. They continue to provide valuable information about MNA operations, including details of the summit delegation's negotiating positions." Vance leaned forward slightly. "Which brings me to the purpose of this briefing. The MNA will use the summit to demand the return of the captured commander. They will offer concessions, perhaps significant ones. The question is what you wish to achieve."

Rowan considered the question. The captured commander was valuable, certainly. A source of intelligence, a bargaining chip, a symbol of Pale City strength. But he was also a liability. Every day he remained in custody was a day the MNA had motivation to conduct another rescue operation. Every day was a day the diplomatic pretense became harder to maintain.

"What is the Quiet Choir's position?"

Vance's expression flickered, the first sign of emotion Rowan had seen. "The Choir believes the prisoner should be used to extract information about Bioweb vulnerabilities. They are eager to continue their research."

"Their research." Rowan's voice hardened. "The Nullwave project."

"Yes."

"The project that was supposed to be dormant. The project that was supposed to be suspended pending review." Rowan stood, unable to contain his agitation. "I received assurances, Vance. After the incident at the Wind Spine, I received explicit assurances that no further tests would be conducted without my authorization."

"The Choir operates with a degree of independence."

"The Choir operates within the structure of this government, and I am the head of this government." Rowan turned to face his intelligence chief. "Are they planning something? Is that why they want the prisoner?"

Vance was silent for a long moment. When he spoke, his voice was even quieter than usual.

"The Choir believes the window for action is closing. The MNA's Bioweb technology continues to advance. Their defensive capabilities grow stronger each year. The Choir's assessment is that if we do not act soon, we may never have another opportunity."

"Act. You mean attack."

"I mean demonstrate capability. Show the MNA that their technology is not invulnerable. Force them to negotiate from a position of weakness rather than strength." Vance stood as well, matching Rowan's intensity with his own cold certainty. "The Nullwave works, Prime Councillor. The test at the Wind Spine proved that. With the information from the captured commander, we can refine the targeting, minimize collateral effects, deliver a strike that will fundamentally alter the balance of power."

Rowan walked to the window. Beyond the glass, Nova-Providence stretched toward the horizon, a forest of towers and spires, ten million people living their lives in the shadow of decisions made in rooms like this one. They believed in the Renewal. They believed in the future the Doctrine Keepers promised. They believed their leaders were protecting them from an enemy that wished to destroy everything they had built.

Some of that was even true.

"I need to think," he said without turning. "The summit resumes in four days. Until then, no action is to be taken regarding the Nullwave. The prisoner is to be held securely but not harmed. And the Choir is to be reminded that their authority derives from this office, not the other way around."

"As you wish." Vance moved toward the door. "There is one other matter."

"Yes?"

"Julienne Drax has requested a meeting. She says it concerns the historical archives and certain... sensitivities regarding the summit negotiations."

Rowan closed his eyes. Drax. Of course. Nothing in this city happened without her awareness, and very little happened without her involvement. If she was requesting a meeting, it meant she had information he needed or demands he would have to accommodate.

"Send her in."

* * *

Julienne Drax entered the chamber like someone who owned

it.

She was a small woman, gray-haired and sharp-featured, with eyes that missed nothing and a manner that suggested she had already anticipated every word you might say. She wore the simple robes of the Doctrine Keepers, unadorned except for the small pin at her collar that marked her rank as Chief Keeper. In a city of elaborate uniforms and status symbols, her simplicity was itself a statement of power.

"Prime Councillor." She did not wait to be offered a seat, settling into the chair Vance had vacated with the ease of long familiarity. "I trust the Assembly was receptive to your address."

"They were appropriately concerned." Rowan returned to his own chair, facing her across the low table. "You said this was about the archives."

"It is about what the archives contain and what the MNA may attempt to use against us during the negotiations." Drax folded her hands in her lap, a gesture that somehow conveyed both patience and menace. "The defector. Elias Harren. He had access to sensitive materials during his time in the Cultural Ministry. Materials that could be damaging if they were to reach MNA hands."

"What kind of materials?"

"Historical records. Original documents from the founding era. Accounts that..." She paused, choosing her words with the precision of someone who understood that words were weapons. "Accounts that differ from the official narrative in ways that could be exploited by our enemies."

Rowan studied her face, looking for the truth beneath the careful phrasing. "You are saying our history is false."

"I am saying our history is *curated*. Every civilization tells stories about itself that serve its needs. The stories we tell are no more or less accurate than anyone else's." Drax's eyes were steady. "But accuracy is not the point. Narrative is the point. And if the MNA can present documents that contradict our narrative, they can undermine the foundations of everything we have built."

"What do you want?"

"Authorization to accelerate the purges. The underground networks that sheltered Harren are still operating. Every day they remain active is a day our vulnerabilities grow." She leaned forward slightly. "I also want assurance that any materials recovered from MNA sources will be directed to my office before being shared with other agencies. The Choir has its own agenda. I would prefer that historical matters remain within the Doctrine Keepers' purview."

Rowan heard what she was not saying. A power struggle between Drax and the Choir, each seeking to control information, each viewing the current crisis as an opportunity to expand their authority. He was the fulcrum between them, the point on which their competing ambitions balanced.

"The purges are already proceeding," he said. "How much more acceleration do you require?"

"Emergency authority. The ability to detain and interrogate without the usual procedural requirements." Drax's voice did not change, but something in her posture sharpened. "The networks are fragmenting. They are moving their people, destroying their records. If we do not act quickly, we will lose the opportunity to eliminate them entirely."

Emergency authority. The power to arrest anyone, question anyone, hold anyone indefinitely without oversight. It was a tool that had been used before, in the early years of the Renewal, when the founders had faced genuine threats to survival. It had been retired precisely because it was too effective, too prone to abuse, too dangerous in the wrong hands.

Drax's hands were precisely the wrong hands.

But the alternative was allowing the underground to survive. Allowing Harren's knowledge to spread. Allowing the cracks in the narrative to widen until the entire structure collapsed.

"Forty-eight hours," Rowan said. "Emergency authority for forty-eight hours, with mandatory review before any extension. All detainees to be documented, all interrogations recorded. And I want daily reports on every action taken under this authorization."

Drax nodded once, the gesture of someone who had gotten exactly what she wanted. "That will be sufficient. I will have the documentation prepared for your signature within the hour."

She rose to leave, then paused at the door. "One more thing, Prime Councillor."

"Yes?"

"The prisoner. The MNA commander. The Choir will want access to him for their research." Her eyes met his. "I would advise against granting that access. The Choir's methods are... effective, but they leave marks. If we intend to use the prisoner as a bargaining chip at the summit, it would be better if he remained presentable."

Rowan heard the warning beneath the advice. Drax was not concerned about the prisoner's welfare. She was concerned about maintaining options, about preserving leverage, about ensuring that the Choir's ambitions did not foreclose diplomatic possibilities.

She was also, whether she realized it or not, giving him

information about the Choir's intentions.

"I will take your advice under consideration," he said.

Drax inclined her head and left. The door closed behind her with a soft click that seemed louder than it should have been.

Rowan sat alone in the private chamber, surrounded by the trappings of power, and thought about the world he had inherited and the world he might leave behind.

* * *

That night, in the residence that had housed every Prime Councillor since the founding, Rowan Halding could not sleep.

He walked the corridors of his private wing, passing portraits of predecessors whose choices had shaped the city he now governed. Men and women who had faced their own impossible decisions, their own moments of crisis, their own temptations to embrace expedience over principle. Some of them were remembered as heroes. Others had been quietly erased from official memory, their failures too damaging to acknowledge.

He wondered which category would claim him.

The Nullwave. The Choir wanted to use it again, wanted to prove that the MNA's technology could be defeated, wanted to shift the balance of power before the window of opportunity closed. Part of him understood the logic. The MNA was stronger than the Pale Cities in almost every meaningful way: more land, more resources, more advanced technology, more unified governance. If that gap continued to widen, eventual conflict would become not just possible but inevitable. And in that conflict, the Pale Cities would lose.

Unless they struck first. Unless they demonstrated capability that would force the MNA to negotiate from weakness. Unless they proved that the Bioweb, for all its wonders, was vulnerable to weapons the Pale Cities had built.

But what would that victory look like? What would remain of the Pale Cities' soul if they won through terror and destruction? The MNA was not an existential threat; they had never sought to conquer or destroy the Pale Cities, only to contain them. The war the Choir imagined was a war of choice, not necessity.

And yet. And yet.

Rowan found himself standing before a door he had not consciously approached. His daughter's room. Marin's room, preserved exactly as she had left it seven years ago, before she had slipped across the border and vanished into MNA territory.

The official story was kidnapping. Brainwashing. A young woman seduced by enemy propaganda, lost to her family and her nation. Rowan had told that story so many times that sometimes he almost believed it.

But he knew the truth. Marin had left because she could no longer live with the lies. She had found documents in his own study, records he had thought were safely hidden, evidence of things the Doctrine Keepers had done in the name of stability. She had confronted him, demanded explanations he could not give, and when he had tried to justify the unjustifiable, she had looked at him with eyes full of something worse than anger.

Disappointment. His daughter had looked at him with disappointment, and then she had left, and he had not heard from her since.

Until three days ago.

The message had come through channels Rowan did not know he still had access to, networks that predated his rise to power, contacts from a younger life when he had believed in things more complicated than survival. His daughter was alive. She wanted to meet. She had information that could change everything.

He had not replied. Had not acknowledged the message. Had told himself that it was a trap, an MNA operation designed to compromise him, a test of loyalties that he could not afford to fail.

But standing here, in the dark corridor outside his daughter's frozen room, Rowan knew that his hesitation had nothing to do with security.

He was afraid.

Afraid of what Marin had become. Afraid of what she might say. Afraid that seeing her would force him to confront the choices he had made, the person he had become, the distance between the man he had imagined himself to be and the man he actually was.

The summit would begin in four days. The Choir was pushing for action. Drax was consolidating power. The underground was being destroyed. And somewhere, across a border that meant everything and nothing, his daughter was waiting for an answer he did not know how to give.

Rowan touched the door of Marin's room. The wood was cool beneath his fingers, unchanged by the years that had passed since she had last opened it.

"I'm sorry," he whispered to the empty corridor. "I'm sorry."

He did not know if he was apologizing for the past or for what he was about to do.

In the morning, he would sign Drax's authorization. He would approve the interrogation of the MNA commander, carefully calibrated to extract information without leaving marks that could not be explained. He would continue the performance of leadership that had become his entire existence.

And he would reply to his daughter's message.

Whatever came of it, whatever trap might be waiting, he needed to know. He needed to see her face and hear her voice and understand what she had become in the years since she had walked away from everything he represented.

He owed her that much.

He owed himself the truth, even if the truth destroyed him.

Rowan Halding, Prime Councillor of the Pale Cities, leader of ten million people, architect of a Cold War that might soon become hot, stood alone in the dark and waited for the dawn.

6

Debts and Silences

Captain Lucian Ford had learned to recognize the weight of surveillance.

It was not something he could see or hear, not exactly. More a texture in the air, a quality of attention that pressed against the skin like humidity before a storm. He felt it now as he walked the corridors of Border Guard headquarters, passing colleagues who nodded with fractionally too much deliberation, whose eyes tracked him a beat longer than courtesy required.

They were watching him. All of them. And they wanted him to know it.

The summons had come at dawn, a formal request for his presence at a security review. Standard procedure following any facility breach, the message had said. All personnel with access to the detention center were being interviewed. Nothing to be concerned about.

Lucian had read those words and understood their opposite meaning. Everything to be concerned about. His name on a list. His actions under scrutiny. The moment he had been dreading for weeks, finally arriving with bureaucratic politeness.

He had helped Renna escape. Months ago, before the summit, before the Cold War had solidified into its current frozen hostility. She had been a prisoner in his custody, and he had looked into her eyes and seen something that made the uniform he wore feel like a costume. He had arranged a transfer that never reached its destination. He had falsified records. He had committed treason, and he had done it without hesitation.

Now someone suspected. Or someone knew. Or someone was fishing, hoping he would reveal himself through the particular nervousness of the guilty.

Lucian kept his pace steady. His expression neutral. His breathing even. He had spent fifteen years in the Border Guard, had faced MNA patrols and underground insurgents and the endless small violences of the frontier. He knew how to control his body when control was all that stood between him and destruction.

The review chamber was in the administrative wing, a windowless room with gray walls and a table bolted to the floor. Three chairs on one side, one on the other. The geometry of interrogation, familiar from training exercises that had always ended with the trainee in the single chair learning exactly how vulnerable isolation could make a person feel.

Two officers waited for him. He recognized both: Major Kellam from Internal Security, a man with a reputation for thoroughness that bordered on obsession, and Lieutenant Varo, a younger officer who served as Kellam's shadow and stenographer. Neither smiled as Lucian entered.

"Captain Ford." Kellam gestured to the single chair. "Thank you for coming."

As if he had been given a choice. Lucian sat, keeping his hands visible on the table, a posture of openness he did not feel.

"This review concerns the events of two nights ago," Kellam continued. "The breach at the Northern Detention Facility. You were on duty that night."

"I was stationed at the eastern checkpoint," Lucian said. "Standard patrol rotation."

"And yet the breach occurred from the west." Kellam's eyes were flat, unreadable. "Your sector was not directly involved in the incursion."

"No, sir."

"Convenient."

Lucian said nothing. Silence was safer than defense. Defense implied guilt.

Kellam consulted a file on the table before him, pages dense with text that Lucian could not read from his angle. "Your service record is exemplary, Captain. Fifteen years. Multiple commendations. Promoted ahead of schedule twice." He turned a page. "And yet there are... anomalies."

"Sir?"

"A prisoner transfer six months ago. A woman named Renna, MNA operative, captured during a border incursion. She was in your custody for transport to a secondary facility. She never arrived." Kellam looked up from the file. "The official report blamed a vehicle malfunction. An opportunity she exploited to escape."

"That is what happened."

"Is it?" Kellam leaned back in his chair. "The vehicle was examined afterward. No malfunction was found. The restraints that should have secured the prisoner were unlocked. And you, Captain, suffered no injuries in the alleged escape, despite being alone with a trained MNA agent."

Lucian's heart was pounding, but he kept his voice level. "I was incapacitated. She struck me from behind. By the time I recovered, she was gone."

"So your report states." Kellam closed the file. "And two nights ago, that same prisoner was extracted from the Northern Facility by MNA operatives. A facility you have accessed multiple times in recent months. A facility whose security protocols you are intimately familiar with."

"As are dozens of other officers."

"But those officers did not lose a prisoner under mysterious circumstances. Those officers have not been flagged by three separate security reviews for behavioral irregularities." Kellam's voice remained calm, almost friendly. "You understand how this appears, Captain."

"I understand that appearance and reality are not the same thing." Lucian met Kellam's eyes directly. "I have served this city my entire adult life. I have risked my life at the border more times than I can count. If you have evidence of wrongdoing, present it. If you have only suspicion, then I respectfully request that this review conclude."

A long silence. Kellam's expression did not change, but something shifted in the quality of his attention. He was recalculating, reassessing, adjusting his approach.

"No evidence," he said finally. "Not yet. But Chief Keeper Drax has been granted emergency authority over internal security matters. The standards for detention have been... relaxed." He stood, and Varo stood with him. "You are free to go, Captain. For now. But I would advise you to consider your position carefully. The city is at war, whether or not that war has been formally declared. Those who are not fully committed to victory may find themselves reclassified."

"Reclassified."

"From asset to liability." Kellam moved toward the door. "Good day, Captain Ford."

They left. The door closed. And Lucian sat alone in the gray room, his hands still flat on the table, his heart still pounding, his mind racing through the implications of everything that had just been said.

They knew. They could not prove it, not yet, but they knew. And Drax's emergency authority meant that proof might soon become optional.

* * *

The barracks were no safer than the corridors.

Lucian returned to his quarters and found them subtly wrong. Nothing missing, nothing obviously disturbed, but the angles were different. His footlocker had been moved a centimeter to the left. The books on his shelf were in a slightly different order. Someone had searched his room, carefully and professionally, looking for evidence that did not exist because Lucian had never been foolish enough to keep any.

He sat on his bunk and stared at the wall and thought about Lena.

His sister had been twelve years old when the fever took her. A common illness, easily treated in the Pale Cities' medical facilities, but Lena had not been in the Pale Cities. She had been in one of the frontier settlements, the marginal communities that clung to the edges of authorized territory, populated by people who had chosen freedom over security. Their parents had been idealists, believers in a different way of living, and Lena had paid the price for their beliefs.

Lucian had been sixteen. He had walked three days to reach the nearest medical station, carrying his sister on his back for the first day and a half, until she became too weak to hold on and he had to carry her in his arms. By the time they arrived, it was too late. The doctors had been kind. They had given Lena a bed and medicine that eased her passing. They had offered Lucian a place at the station, an education, a path into the Border Guard that protected citizens from the dangers his parents had embraced.

He had accepted. He had become a model officer. He had served with distinction and never questioned orders and told himself that the system he enforced was just, was necessary, was the only thing standing between civilization and chaos.

And then he had met Renna.

She had been injured when they captured her, a wound in her side that should have received immediate treatment but instead had been left to fester while she was processed through the intake system. Lucian had been assigned to transport her to the detention facility, and somewhere on that journey, she had started talking. Not propaganda, not defiance, just... talking. About her home. About the forests that grew in patterns guided by human intention. About the animals that worked alongside people rather than serving them. About a world where technology healed rather than extracted.

She had reminded him of Lena. Not in appearance, not in personality, but in something harder to name. A quality of presence. A way of looking at the world that assumed it could be better than it was.

He had not planned to help her escape. He had not made a conscious decision to betray everything he had spent his life building. He had simply looked at her in the back of the transport vehicle, looked at the facility waiting to receive her, and known that he could not deliver her to that place. Could not watch another person who reminded him of his sister disappear into a system designed to break her.

The falsified records had come later. The cover story about the vehicle malfunction. The careful construction of a lie that had held for six months and was now beginning to crumble.

Lucian had no illusions about what would happen if they caught him. The detention facilities he had helped staff for fifteen years would become his home. The interrogation techniques he had witnessed would be applied to his own body. And eventually, when they had extracted everything he knew, he would disappear into the category of people who had never existed.

He should run. He should use the contacts he had carefully cultivated, the underground networks he had learned about through years of hunting them, and disappear before Drax's authority could close around him.

But running would confirm their suspicions. Running would expose the people who had helped him. Running would mean abandoning the one asset he still had: his position inside the system, his access to information the MNA desperately needed.

And there was the new prisoner to consider. The MNA commander captured during the extraction. Lucian had seen the transfer orders, had recognized the name from intelligence briefings. A senior officer with decades of experience, now in Pale City hands, facing the same fate Lucian had saved Renna from.

He could help. He could use what remained of his access to gather information, to pass warnings, to give the MNA a chance to rescue their commander before the Quiet Choir's methods destroyed him.

Or he could try, and fail, and die in a gray room with no one knowing what he had attempted.

Lucian stood and moved to the small desk beneath his window. The window looked out on the exercise yard, empty now in the evening light, but he knew there were cameras tracking the view, recording anyone who might signal or receive signals from outside. He kept his back to the window as he opened the desk drawer and retrieved a worn notebook.

The notebook was innocent. Personal reflections, observations about weather and wildlife, the kind of private journal many soldiers kept to maintain their sanity during long deployments. But scattered through its pages were phrases that meant something different to those who knew how to read them. Contact points. Emergency protocols. The skeleton of a communication network that had been built over years by people who had grown tired of serving lies.

He found the page he needed and memorized the sequence it contained. Then he closed the notebook, returned it to the drawer, and walked out of his quarters with the careful casualness of a man with nothing to hide.

* * *

The dead drop was in the industrial sector, a maintenance junction where pipes from the recycling facilities intersected with the city's water reclamation system.

Lucian had used it twice before, both times to pass information that had seemed urgent at the moment and trivial in retrospect. Patrol schedules. Facility layouts. The kind of intelligence that kept the underground alive but rarely changed anything. He had never used it for something that mattered.

Tonight would be different.

He took a circuitous route, doubling back twice, stopping at shops and food vendors to establish a pattern of normal behavior. The surveillance on him would be looking for anomalies, for deviations from routine. He gave them none. He was just a man walking home after a difficult day, stopping for a meal, taking the long way because the evening air was pleasant.

The junction was accessed through a service door that required a maintenance code. Lucian had the code because he had made a point of collecting such things, small keys to small doors that might someday prove useful. He entered quickly, closed the door behind him, and waited for his eyes to adjust to the darkness.

The dead drop was a hollow space behind a junction box, invisible unless you knew exactly where to look. Lucian retrieved the small container he had prepared in his quarters, a waterproof case containing a paper message that would dissolve if exposed to moisture. Old technology. Untrackable technology. The kind of communication the Signal Mesh could not intercept.

The message was simple. Three sentences that contained everything he could safely convey.

They know about the safe houses. Move everyone. The commander is in the secondary facility.

He placed the container in the hollow space and sealed it. Someone would check within twenty-four hours. Someone would pass the message along the chain. And somewhere, if luck held, people who were about to be arrested would instead be warned. People who were planning a rescue would know where to look.

It was not much. It might not be enough. But it was what he could do without exposing himself completely, and for now, that would have to be enough.

He left the junction and resumed his walk home, his pace unhurried, his expression unremarkable. Around him, the city hummed with its evening routines: workers returning from shifts, families gathering for meals, the Signal Mesh playing its endless soundtrack of reassurance and subtle threat. He was invisible in the crowd, one face among millions, a man whose interior life was a treason the system could not see.

Kellam's words echoed in his mind. *Those who are not fully committed to victory may find themselves reclassified.* Asset to liability. Citizen to prisoner. Person to unperson.

Lucian had crossed a line years ago, the night he let Renna go. Every day since had been borrowed time, a reprieve that could end at any moment. He had known this. Had accepted it. Had told himself that the risk was worth taking because some things mattered more than survival.

But knowing and feeling were different things. And tonight, walking through the city that had raised him and trained him and made him into a weapon it would soon turn against itself, Lucian felt the weight of his choices pressing down with a gravity that threatened to crush him.

He thought about the commander in the detention facility. A man he had never met, whose name he knew only from reports, who was at this moment experiencing the same helplessness Lucian had seen in Renna's eyes. The same slow destruction that the Pale Cities called interrogation and the MNA called torture and the Quiet Choir called research.

He could not save that man alone. Could not storm the facility, could not fight his way through security, could not do anything except what he had done: leave a message in a dead drop and hope that people more capable than himself would find a way.

But perhaps there was something more he could do. Something that used his position instead of abandoning it.

Kellam suspected him. Drax was watching. Every move he made would be scrutinized. But if he could maintain his cover, if he could continue to appear loyal while feeding information to the underground, he might be able to do more than leave messages in hollow spaces.

He might be able to help from the inside when the MNA came for their commander.

It was a dangerous thought. A foolish thought. The kind of thought that got people killed in gray rooms with no one to mourn them.

But Lucian had been foolish before, had helped Renna when wisdom demanded he look away, and he was still alive. Still useful. Still capable of making choices that mattered.

He reached his quarters as the last light faded from the sky. The room was exactly as he had left it, the subtle wrongness of the earlier search already fading into familiarity. He sat on his bunk and closed his eyes and thought about Lena, about Renna, about the commander whose name he had memorized and whose face he had never seen.

Tomorrow, he would report for duty. He would wear the uniform and follow orders and pretend to be the loyal officer everyone believed him to be. He would watch for opportunities and wait for the message that would tell him his warning had been received.

And when the time came, if the time came, he would be ready to choose again.

Asset or liability. Citizen or prisoner. Person or unperson.

Lucian Ford had already made his choice. Now he just had to survive long enough for it to matter.

7

The Summit Opens

The trading post had been built for commerce, not diplomacy.

It sat on the border like an afterthought, a sprawl of weathered buildings that had once served as the primary exchange point between two worlds. Before the Cold War solidified, before the rhetoric hardened into policy, people had come here to trade goods and stories and the small intimacies that made neighbors of strangers. Pale City merchants had bartered manufactured goods for MNA crops and medicines. Children from both sides had played together in the dusty streets while their parents negotiated prices.

That was decades ago. Now the trading post stood mostly empty, its warehouses hollow, its streets patrolled by guards from both factions who watched each other with the particular wariness of people trained to see enemies everywhere. The commerce that had once flowed through this place had dried up, diverted to official channels controlled by officials who understood that trade was another form of warfare.

Chogan Grayfeather remembered the old days. He had been young then, an apprentice diplomat accompanying his mentor to negotiations that had seemed consequential at the time but now revealed themselves as the last gasps of a dying peace. He had believed, in those years, that understanding between peoples was possible. That conversation could bridge any divide. That the arc of history bent toward connection rather than conflict.

He no longer believed that. But he had not stopped trying.

The summit delegation had arrived at dawn, a procession of diplomats and advisors and security personnel that transformed the empty trading post into something resembling a capital. MNA banners hung from the buildings assigned to them, fabric woven with patterns that told stories older than any nation. Pale City flags flew from the opposite side of the central plaza, their geometric designs speaking a different language of power and precision.

Between them, the neutral ground waited. A single building, larger than the others, where the actual negotiations would take place. Its walls had been stripped of all decoration, all allegiance, all history. A blank space where two incompatible visions of the future would try to find common ground.

Chogan stood at the window of his assigned quarters and watched the Pale City delegation arrive. Their vehicles were angular and loud, burning fuel in a display of abundance that was also a statement of philosophy. We do not need to conserve. We do not need to balance. We take what we require and build what we want.

The lead vehicle disgorged a figure Chogan recognized from intelligence briefings: Undersecretary Varn, a career diplomat with a reputation for inflexibility masked by surface courtesy. Not Prime Councillor Halding himself. The Pale Cities were sending their second tier, a signal that they did not expect these negotiations to produce meaningful results.

Or a signal that they wanted the MNA to believe that, while something else happened elsewhere.

"You are thinking too hard." The voice came from behind him, familiar and welcome. "I can hear it from across the room."

Chogan turned. Elder Mirova stood in the doorway, her silver hair bound in the intricate patterns of the Northern Nations, her face carrying the particular combination of wisdom and weariness that came from a lifetime of trying to prevent wars. She had been his mentor once, long ago. Now she served as senior advisor to the delegation, a role that meant she could say things Chogan could not.

"I am thinking about what they are not showing us," he said. "The delegation is smaller than expected. Their security presence is lighter than protocol demands. Either they are confident or they are distracted."

"Or they want us to wonder which." Mirova moved to stand beside him at the window. "Diplomacy is theater, Chogan. You taught me that, or perhaps I taught you. I can no longer remember."

"You taught me. I merely learned poorly."

She smiled, the expression brief and tired. "The Council has sent instructions. They want you to open with a demand for Commander Speaks-Low's return. Immediate and unconditional."

"They know the Pale Cities will refuse."

"Of course. The demand is not meant to succeed. It is meant to establish position, to demonstrate resolve, to show our people that we have not abandoned our commander." Mirova's voice carried a note of something that might have been frustration. "Politics performed for an audience that is not in the room."

"And while we perform, Speaks-Low remains in their custody."

"Yes."

Chogan turned away from the window. The weight of it pressed on him, the gap between what diplomacy could achieve and what the moment required. He had argued for a different approach, had suggested that the extraction operation be postponed until the summit could establish a framework for negotiation. He had been overruled. The rescue had proceeded, had succeeded partially, had left Speaks-Low in enemy hands and the Cold War colder than ever.

Now he was expected to negotiate as if none of that had happened. As if the bodies of Talon and River-Runs-Deep were not being prepared for burial. As if Kele was not lying broken in a medical ward. As if the friend he had known for thirty years was not at this moment being subjected to interrogations designed to shatter the human mind.

"There is other news," Mirova said quietly. "From the border network."

"Elias?"

"The safe houses have been evacuated. The warning arrived in time. Most of the network has survived the purges." She paused. "He is still requesting extraction. The Council has authorized the operation to proceed during the summit window."

"Aiyana is leading it."

"Yes. She departed last night with a small team. They will approach through the eastern corridor while attention is focused here." Mirova's eyes met his. "The Council believes the risk is acceptable."

"The Council is not the one taking the risk." Chogan heard the bitterness in his own voice and did not try to soften it. "We send our young people into danger while we sit in comfortable rooms and debate acceptable losses."

"That is the nature of leadership. You know this."

"I know it. I do not accept it." He moved toward the door. "When does the session begin?"

"Two hours. Time enough to prepare, to review the briefings, to compose the mask you will need to wear." Mirova touched his arm as he passed. "Chogan. I know this is difficult. I know you feel responsible for what happened. But the work continues. It must continue. Because if we stop talking, the only language left is violence."

He paused at the door. "We are already speaking in violence. We simply pretend otherwise."

"Then we pretend. Because pretense is sometimes the only thing standing between cold war and hot."

He left without responding. There was nothing to say that would not sound like surrender.

* * *

The negotiating chamber had been designed for neutrality, but neutrality was its own kind of statement.

The walls were bare stone, unworked, untouched by either MNA cultivation or Pale City manufacture. The furniture was wood of uncertain origin, neither grown nor built, simply old. Light entered through skylights that had been cleaned until they were transparent, neither tinted nor filtered, allowing the raw sun to fall without interpretation.

Two delegations faced each other across a table long enough to prevent casual conversation. Chogan sat at the center of the MNA side, flanked by advisors and translators and observers whose presence was required by protocol if not by necessity. Across from him, Undersecretary Varn arranged his papers with the deliberate precision of someone who wanted his composure noted.

"Elder Grayfeather." Varn's voice was smooth, cultured, carrying the accent of Nova-Providence's elite districts. "Thank you for agreeing to continue these discussions despite recent... complications."

"Undersecretary Varn." Chogan kept his own voice equally measured. "We are always prepared to discuss matters of mutual concern. Though I confess surprise that Prime Councillor Halding chose not to attend personally."

"The Prime Councillor's schedule is demanding. The aftermath of your attack on our facility has required significant attention." Varn smiled, the expression empty of warmth. "I am fully authorized to negotiate on his behalf."

"Our rescue operation," Chogan corrected mildly. "Of prisoners held illegally under violations of the territorial accords."

"Terrorists detained lawfully after crossing our borders without authorization." Varn's smile did not waver. "But perhaps we should not begin with points of disagreement. There will be time enough for those."

Chogan inclined his head, acknowledging the rhetorical parry. This was how it always went. Each side restating positions that could not be reconciled, each pretending that enough words might somehow bridge the unbridgeable. The dance of diplomacy, performed for audiences who needed to believe their leaders were trying.

"The Many Nations Alliance has several concerns we wish to address," he said. "Chief among them is the status of

Commander Speaks-Low, who was taken captive during the incident at your facility. We request his immediate return, along with assurances regarding his treatment during his detention."

"Ah." Varn made a note on his paper. "The individual you refer to was captured while conducting an armed assault on sovereign Pale City territory. He is currently being held pending investigation into his crimes. His treatment is consistent with our legal standards for such cases."

"Your legal standards include interrogation techniques that violate every principle of humane treatment."

"Our legal standards are our own concern." Varn's voice hardened slightly, the first crack in his diplomatic polish. "As are the methods your operatives used to breach our security and kill three of our citizens."

"Those deaths are regrettable. They were not our intention."

"And yet they occurred. Intention does not resurrect the dead." Varn set down his pen. "Elder Grayfeather, we can continue this exchange of accusations indefinitely. Each side has grievances. Each side has justifications. But I wonder if there might be a more productive use of our time."

Chogan studied the man across the table. There was something beneath the surface, a current that did not match the expected patterns. Varn was supposed to be a hardliner, a true believer in Pale City supremacy, a man who viewed the MNA as obstacles to be overcome rather than partners to be engaged. Yet his words suggested something else. An opening, perhaps. Or a trap.

"What did you have in mind?" Chogan asked carefully.

"An exchange." Varn glanced at his own delegation, a signal Chogan could not interpret. "You want your commander returned. We want certain assurances regarding your technology. Specifically, the Bioweb systems that power your infrastructure."

"You want us to share our technology."

"I want us to discuss the possibility. Not transfer of the technology itself, necessarily, but an understanding of its capabilities and limitations." Varn leaned forward slightly. "The Quiet Choir has developed weapons that can disrupt harmonic frequencies. You know this. The test at the Wind Spine demonstrated the principle. What you may not know is that those weapons are being refined. Improved. Prepared for deployment on a larger scale."

The words hung in the air. Around the table, both delegations had gone still, recognizing that something had shifted, that the performance of diplomacy had suddenly become something more dangerous.

"You are threatening us," Chogan said quietly.

"I am informing you. There is a difference." Varn's expression had not changed, but his eyes carried a weight that his words could not fully convey. "There are factions within our government that believe the time for negotiation has passed. They see your technology as an existential threat and believe the only solution is to neutralize that threat before it grows beyond our capacity to counter. They are preparing to act. Soon."

"And you are telling us this because…?"

"Because I am not one of those factions." Varn lowered his voice, the words meant for Chogan alone despite the audience surrounding them. "Because I believe that a war between our peoples would destroy us both. And because the only way to prevent that war is for both sides to step back from the edge before we fall."

Chogan sat with the implications, weighing them against everything he knew about Pale City politics, about the Quiet Choir, about the weapons that had already damaged the Bioweb in ways that might never fully heal.

"What are you proposing?" he asked.

"A private conversation. Tonight, after the formal sessions end. Just the two of us, without advisors, without protocols, without the need to perform for our respective audiences." Varn's eyes held his. "I have information you need. You have assurances I can carry back to those who might still be persuaded. Perhaps together we can find a path that does not lead to destruction."

It was irregular. It was potentially a trap. It was exactly the kind of back-channel communication that could undermine everything the formal summit was meant to achieve.

It was also, possibly, the only hope.

"Tonight," Chogan said. "After the evening meal. I will find you."

Varn nodded once, then straightened in his chair, resuming his public persona. "Now then. Shall we continue with the official agenda? I believe we have several hours of productive disagreement ahead of us."

The formal session continued. Words exchanged, positions restated, the careful choreography of diplomatic stalemate. But beneath the surface, something had changed. A possibility had opened, fragile and uncertain, a crack in the wall between worlds.

Chogan participated in the performance while his mind worked elsewhere, calculating risks, weighing options, wondering whether Varn's words were a genuine offer or an elaborate deception.

Somewhere beyond these walls, Aiyana was moving through enemy territory, pursuing an extraction that might succeed or might end in disaster. Somewhere, Speaks-Low was enduring interrogation. Somewhere, the Quiet Choir was preparing weapons that could kill the land itself.

And here, in a room designed for neutrality, two men who should have been enemies were reaching toward something that might be understanding.

Chogan did not know if it would be enough. He suspected it would not.

But he had spent his life trying to prevent the unpreventable, speaking words into voids that swallowed them without echo. He would try again tonight. He would listen to what Varn had to say. He would search for the path that did not lead to destruction.

And if he failed, if the war came anyway, at least he would know that he had tried.

The sun moved across the skylights, marking time in the way it had for centuries, indifferent to the small creatures below who thought their conflicts mattered. The session continued. The words accumulated. And the border that had been quiet for so long held its breath, waiting to see which way the balance would finally tip.

* * *

That evening, as the delegations retired to their respective quarters, a message reached Chogan through the network's secure channels.

He read it in the privacy of his room, the words brief and encoded, their meaning clear only to those who knew the cipher.

Package in transit. Eastern corridor. Expected arrival: three days.

Aiyana was moving. Elias would be extracted. In three days, they would either have their asset safely across the border or they would have another disaster to add to the growing list.

Chogan burned the message and watched the ashes dissolve into nothing.

Then he went to find Undersecretary Varn, to hear what a Pale City diplomat was willing to say when no one else was listening.

The trading post was quiet around him, its empty streets holding the ghosts of commerce that would never return. Above, the stars emerged in a sky that belonged to neither nation, that had watched civilizations rise and fall and rise again, that would continue watching long after the current conflict had become another layer of sediment in the geological record of human folly.

Chogan walked through that ancient indifference toward a conversation that might change nothing or might change everything.

He had learned long ago not to hope. Hope was a luxury that diplomats could not afford.

But he had not learned to stop trying. That, perhaps, was its own form of hope, disguised as duty.

The door to Varn's quarters stood slightly open, light spilling into the corridor like an invitation or a trap.

Chogan entered.

And the summit, the real summit, finally began.

8

What Cannot Be Said

Varn's quarters were spartan in a way that surprised Chogan.

He had expected the opulence that Pale City officials typically affected: heavy furniture, elaborate decorations, the material abundance that their culture treated as proof of worth. Instead, he found a room almost as bare as the negotiating chamber, furnished with only the essentials and devoid of personal effects. A soldier's room, not a diplomat's.

"You seem surprised." Varn stood by the window, his formal jacket removed, his posture looser than it had been during the official session. "Did you expect silk curtains and gold fixtures?"

"I expected something," Chogan admitted. "This feels like a man who does not intend to stay long."

"Perceptive." Varn gestured to a chair. "Please. This conversation may take some time, and I prefer we both be comfortable."

Chogan sat. The chair was hard, functional, designed for utility rather than comfort. Everything in this room was a message, he realized. Varn was presenting himself as something other than what his position suggested.

"You said you have information," Chogan began. "And that you want assurances. Perhaps we should start with what you are offering."

Varn moved away from the window and sat across from him, leaning forward with his elbows on his knees. The posture was deliberate, Chogan knew. Everything about this man was deliberate. But the words that followed had the weight of something genuine.

"The Quiet Choir has completed development of the Nullwave device. Not the prototype that was tested at the Wind Spine. A full-scale weapon, capable of affecting a region hundreds of kilometers across." Varn's eyes held Chogan's. "They intend to use it within the month."

The words landed like stones in still water, their implications rippling outward. Chogan kept his expression neutral, though his mind was racing through scenarios, each worse than the last.

"Where?"

"The target has not been finalized. There are factions arguing for different approaches." Varn paused. "Some want to strike at your industrial capacity. Others prefer a demonstration against civilian infrastructure. A few are advocating for an attack on the Bioweb's central nodes, which they believe would collapse your entire network."

"All of those options would kill thousands of people."

"Directly, perhaps fewer than you think. The Nullwave does not kill humans directly. It kills the systems you depend on." Varn's voice was flat, clinical. "But the secondary effects: the collapse of medical facilities, the failure of food distribution, the breakdown of the harmonic networks that regulate your environment. Yes. Thousands would die. Perhaps more."

Chogan felt a cold certainty settling in his chest. This was not a negotiating tactic. This was not a threat designed to extract concessions. This was a man describing a catastrophe he believed was imminent and unstoppable.

"Why are you telling me this?"

"Because I do not want it to happen." Varn stood abruptly, moving to the window again, staring out at the darkness beyond. "I have spent my career believing that the Pale Cities represented something worth preserving. A different path. An alternative to the MNA's way of living. But the path the Choir is proposing is not preservation. It is destruction."

"You could stop them."

"No." The word was sharp, final. "I do not have that power. The Choir operates outside normal chains of command. They answer to ideologues, not politicians. Even Prime Councillor Halding has limited control over their actions." He turned to face Chogan. "But I can warn you. And I can tell you that there are others within our government who share my concerns. We are not a unified bloc of warmongers, whatever your propaganda suggests."

"What do you want in return for this warning?"

"Assurances. Evidence that the MNA is willing to find a path forward that does not require the Choir's weapons." Varn's voice softened. "If I can bring back proof that negotiation is possible, that your people are willing to discuss terms that address our legitimate concerns, I may be able to strengthen the faction that opposes the Choir. Buy time. Perhaps prevent the attack altogether."

"What terms?"

"Technology sharing. Not the Bioweb itself, but knowledge.

Understanding of how your systems work, so that we can adapt our own infrastructure. Trade agreements that give us access to resources we currently lack. And..." Varn hesitated. "Recognition."

"Recognition of what?"

"Of our right to exist. Of the Pale Cities as a legitimate society, not an aberration to be corrected or a cancer to be excised." His voice carried an edge now, something personal beneath the diplomatic facade. "Your people speak of us as if we are a disease. As if our existence is an affront to the natural order. The Doctrine Keepers use that rhetoric to justify their own crimes, but the perception is not entirely invented. We feel your contempt, Elder Grayfeather. We feel it in every negotiation, every treaty, every carefully worded communique that treats us as problems rather than people."

Chogan was quiet for a long moment. The accusation was uncomfortable precisely because it contained truth. The MNA did view the Pale Cities as a failing, a wrong turn in history that had persisted long past the point where it should have been corrected. Even those who advocated for peace often framed it as patience with a child who would eventually learn better.

"You are asking us to validate a society built on extraction and exploitation," he said carefully. "A society that has caused immeasurable harm to the land and continues to do so."

"I am asking you to acknowledge that we are human beings with the right to determine our own future. Even if that future looks different from yours." Varn returned to his chair, sitting heavily, suddenly looking older than his years. "The Choir believes you will never grant that acknowledgment. They believe war is inevitable because the MNA will never accept the Pale Cities as equals. They use that belief to justify their weapons."

"And if they are right?"

"Then we are all lost." Varn met his eyes. "But I do not believe they are right. I believe there are people on both sides who understand that coexistence is the only alternative to mutual destruction. I believe you are one of those people, Elder Grayfeather. That is why I asked for this conversation."

Chogan considered the man before him. Everything he knew about Pale City officials suggested caution, suggested that any offer was a trap, suggested that trust was a weapon to be used against those naive enough to extend it. But Varn's words had the texture of sincerity, and his warning about the Nullwave aligned with intelligence the MNA had gathered through other channels.

"I cannot make the assurances you are asking for," he said finally. "That authority rests with the Rooted Council, and they will not act on the word of one diplomat in a private meeting."

"I understand."

"But I can carry your words back to them. I can advocate for a response that addresses your concerns without surrendering our principles." Chogan leaned forward. "And I can tell you something in return. Something that may help you in your own internal struggles."

Varn waited, his expression wary but attentive.

"There are people within your government who have been communicating with us. Not spies. Not traitors in the sense your Doctrine Keepers would define. People who believe, as you seem to believe, that the current path leads to catastrophe." Chogan chose his next words carefully. "One of those people has been trying to reach Prime Councillor Halding directly. To warn him about the Choir's intentions and offer information that might help him contain them."

Varn's expression shifted, surprise breaking through his diplomatic composure. "Who?"

"I cannot tell you that. But I can tell you that the message has been sent, and we are waiting to see if he responds." Chogan stood, signaling that the conversation was nearing its end. "If the Prime Councillor is truly interested in preventing the Choir's attack, he has channels through which to communicate. We are listening."

"You are taking a risk, telling me this."

"We are all taking risks. That is what this moment requires." Chogan moved toward the door. "The formal sessions will continue tomorrow. We will make our demands, you will make your refusals, and the theater of diplomacy will proceed. But beneath that theater, perhaps something real is happening. Perhaps not. We will see."

"Elder Grayfeather." Varn's voice stopped him at the door. "There is one more thing."

Chogan turned.

"Your commander. The one we captured." Varn's face was troubled. "The Choir has been pressing for access to him. They want to interrogate him about Bioweb vulnerabilities. So far, the Prime Councillor has resisted, but the pressure is increasing."

"And?"

"And I do not know how much longer he can resist. If the Choir gains access, if they use their methods on your commander..." Varn shook his head. "Whatever information he possesses, they will extract it. And whatever remains of him afterward will not be the man you knew."

Chogan felt the weight of those words settle into his bones.

Speaks-Low, whom he had known for thirty years. Speaks-Low, who had trained generations of Guardians and served with more distinction than anyone in the Alliance. Speaks-Low, now sitting in a cell somewhere, waiting for interrogators who would take everything from him and leave nothing behind.

"How much time?" he asked, his voice rougher than he intended.

"Days. Perhaps less. The Choir is not patient, and they sense that the political winds are shifting in their favor." Varn's eyes held genuine sympathy. "I am sorry. I wish I had better news."

Chogan nodded once, not trusting himself to speak. Then he opened the door and stepped out into the corridor, leaving Varn alone with whatever demons haunted men who tried to serve two masters.

**

The night air was cold against his face as Chogan walked the empty streets of the trading post.

He did not return to his quarters. He could not face the walls, the ceiling, the small enclosed space where thoughts would circle without resolution. Instead, he walked toward the edge of the settlement, toward the place where the buildings ended and the border began.

The border was invisible here. No fence, no wall, no physical marker to show where one world ended and another began. Just an imaginary line drawn on maps by people who believed that lines could contain reality. On one side, MNA territory: land that had been tended for generations, forests and fields and rivers that flowed according to patterns humans and nature had negotiated together. On the other side, Pale City territory: land that had been used and exhausted, its resources extracted, its balance broken.

Chogan stood at that invisible boundary and stared into the darkness beyond.

The Nullwave. A weapon that could kill the Bioweb itself, that could silence the song that connected every living thing in MNA territory. He had known it existed; the incident at the Wind Spine had proven that. But a full-scale weapon, ready for deployment, targeted at his people...

He thought about what Varn had asked for. Recognition. Legitimacy. The acknowledgment that the Pale Cities had a right to exist on their own terms.

Could the MNA give that? Could they accept a society that violated everything they believed about the relationship between humans and the land? Could they validate extraction, pollution, the systematic destruction of ecosystems, simply because the people committing those acts were human beings with human rights?

The answer should have been no. The MNA's entire philosophy rested on the principle that some ways of living were sustainable and others were not, that the measure of a society was its relationship with the world that sustained it. The Pale Cities had failed that measure. They continued to fail it. Acknowledging their legitimacy felt like acknowledging that failure did not matter.

And yet.

And yet ten million people lived in Nova-Providence alone. Tens of millions more in the other Pale Cities. Human beings with families, with dreams, with the same capacity for love and loss and hope that MNA citizens possessed. Were they to be written off as collateral damage in a war of philosophies? Were their children responsible for the choices their ancestors had made?

Chogan had spent his life believing that the answer to conflict was understanding. That if people talked long enough, honestly enough, they could find common ground. That war was a failure of imagination, not an inevitability.

Standing here, at the edge of everything, he was no longer certain.

Varn had seemed sincere. But sincerity was not enough. Even if he genuinely wanted peace, he was one voice among many, a moderate in a government increasingly dominated by extremists. The Quiet Choir had weapons. Drax had propaganda. Halding had fear. What did the moderates have except good intentions and diminishing time?

And on the MNA side, what did Chogan have? A Council that debated while crises escalated. A young Guardian leading an extraction that might succeed or might fail. A captured commander who might break before anyone could reach him. A traitor somewhere in the ranks, feeding information to enemies who used it to spring traps.

We are all pretending, he thought. Pretending this can hold. Pretending that words can do what actions cannot. Pretending that the border between cold war and hot is anything more than a breath, a moment, a single decision made by someone who has stopped believing in alternatives.

The stars wheeled overhead, indifferent to the small dramas unfolding beneath them. Somewhere in the distance, an owl called, hunting in the space between nations, unconcerned with the territories humans had drawn.

Chogan stood at the border until the cold became unbearable. Then he turned and walked back toward the trading post, toward the pretense of diplomacy, toward the morning that would bring another day of careful words masking desperate fears.

He composed his message to the Council as he walked. The Nullwave weapon. Varn's offer. The narrow window in which intervention might still be possible. He would send it before dawn, coded and encrypted, trusting that it would reach the right people in time for them to act.

Whether they would act was another question. Whether action would matter was another still.

But he would try. That was all he had ever done. Try, and fail, and try again, and hope that somewhere in the accumulation of failed attempts, something would finally take hold.

The trading post swallowed him back into its empty streets. Tomorrow, the summit would resume. The theater would continue. And beneath the theater, in the spaces where truth lived, the war that had been building for generations would continue its slow, inexorable advance.

Chogan Grayfeather, Elder and diplomat, servant of a peace that might already be lost, returned to his quarters and began to write.

The message was long. The night was longer. And when dawn finally came, gray and uncertain over the mountains, he sent his words into the void and waited to see if anyone was listening.

9

What the River Carries

One week after the extraction, Kele finally spoke.

Aiyana had visited him every day since returning from the summit briefings, sitting in the quiet of his room in the grandmother oak while healers moved through their gentle routines and the Bioweb hummed its frequencies of repair. He had not acknowledged her presence for most of those visits, his eyes fixed on distances that existed only in his damaged mind, his body present but his consciousness somewhere else entirely.

The healers called it retreat. A natural response to trauma, they said, the mind protecting itself by withdrawing from a reality that had become unbearable. They assured Aiyana that he would return when he was ready, that forcing engagement would only deepen the harm. She had nodded and accepted their wisdom and sat with him anyway, because being present was the only thing she could offer.

Today, his eyes found her.

She was sitting by the window, watching the afternoon light filter through leaves that had begun to turn with the season's change, when she felt the quality of the room shift. Something in the air, in the Bioweb's subtle harmonics, in the way the silence had suddenly become a different kind of silence.

She turned. Kele was looking at her. Actually looking, not through her or past her but at her, his gaze carrying the particular weight of someone who has returned from a long journey.

"Aiyana." His voice was rough, unused, but it was his voice. "You came for me."

"I came for you." She moved to the chair beside his bed, the one she had occupied for hours each day, waiting for this moment. "How do you feel?"

The question was inadequate, and they both knew it. How did anyone feel after what he had experienced? There were no words in any language that could contain that answer.

"I feel..." He paused, searching for truth among the rubble of his thoughts. "I feel like I am still there. In the room where they asked questions. Even now, part of me is still in that room."

"You are safe now. You are home."

"I know." His eyes drifted toward the window, toward the green world beyond the glass. "I know I am safe. The knowing does not reach all the way down." He was quiet for a moment, then continued, his voice steadier. "They wanted to understand the Bioweb. How it works. How it connects. They had questions I did not know how to answer, and they did not believe me when I said I did not know."

"You do not have to talk about this."

"I need to talk about it." His hands gripped the blanket that covered him, knuckles whitening. "I need someone to know. I need to put the words outside of me, so they are not only inside."

Aiyana nodded and waited. This was his story to tell at his own pace.

"They had a device," Kele said. "Something that generated frequencies. Discordant frequencies, like the Bioweb singing wrong. When they used it, I could feel the wrongness in my bones. In my mind." He shuddered. "They would turn it on and ask questions, and when I could not answer, they would increase the intensity. It was like... like being unmade. Like the parts of me that fit together were being pulled apart."

Aiyana felt cold spread through her chest. She had heard rumors of such technology, whispers from the intelligence services about Quiet Choir experiments. But hearing it described by someone who had experienced it was different. Worse.

"They called it tuning," Kele continued. "Like I was an instrument they were trying to play. They said that if I would just tell them what they wanted to know, they would stop. They said they did not want to hurt me. They just needed to understand." His laugh was hollow, broken. "As if understanding and hurting were different things. As if taking apart a living mind to see how it works is not the same as destroying it."

"What did they want to know?"

"Everything. The resonance frequencies that power our technology. The way the Bioweb connects to living things. The vulnerabilities in the network." Kele met her eyes. "They were looking for weaknesses, Aiyana. Ways to attack the Bioweb more effectively. The Wind Spine incident was just a test. They are planning something larger."

"We know. Intelligence has confirmed that the Nullwave is being prepared for deployment."

"Then they succeeded." His voice cracked. "They succeeded

because I talked. I do not remember what I told them. There are gaps, holes where memories should be. But I know I talked. I could not help it. The tuning broke something, and words came out that I could not stop."

"Kele." Aiyana reached out, touching his arm gently. "Whatever you told them, it was not your fault. They used methods designed to break any person. There is no shame in being broken by the unbreakable."

"There is shame." His voice was barely a whisper. "There will always be shame. I knew things. Things that could help them hurt us. And now they have those things because I could not hold on."

Aiyana did not argue. She knew that words of comfort would not reach the place where his guilt lived. That place was too deep, too raw, too recently wounded. All she could do was sit with him and let him know he was not alone.

They sat in silence for a long time. Outside, birds called to each other in the branches of the grandmother oak, their songs carrying through the healing frequencies of the tree. The world continued its turning, indifferent to the small tragedies unfolding within its embrace.

"There is something else," Kele said finally. "Something I need to tell you."

"What?"

"The questions they asked. Some of them were too specific. Too targeted." He turned to face her fully, and she saw the intelligence that still lived behind the damage, the analytical mind that had made him valuable enough to interrogate. "They knew things about our systems that they should not have known. Technical details. Operational patterns. The kinds of things that only someone with deep access to MNA infrastructure would understand."

Aiyana felt the confirmation of what Renna had told her, another piece of evidence pointing toward the same terrible conclusion.

"You think they have a source inside the Alliance."

"I know they do." Kele's voice was certain despite his fragility. "The things they knew, Aiyana. The specific questions they asked about Bioweb node configurations, about the harmonic frequencies we use for long-distance communication, about the vulnerabilities in our eastern network infrastructure. That information does not exist in any document they could have captured. It exists only in the minds of people who work with those systems daily."

"Can you identify who might have that knowledge?"

"A dozen people, maybe more. Engineers, administrators, Council advisors with technical clearance." He shook his head. "I have been lying here trying to narrow it down, but I cannot. The information was too broad, touching too many areas. Either they have multiple sources, or they have someone very highly placed."

Aiyana thought about the implications. A traitor with high-level access. Multiple traitors working together. Either possibility was devastating. Either meant that no operation was secure, no plan could be trusted, no communication could be considered private.

"I have to tell the Council," she said.

"Be careful who you tell." Kele's grip on her arm tightened. "If the traitor is highly placed, they may be in a position to intercept any report you make. They may be someone you trust."

The words hung in the air between them, heavy with implications that neither wanted to speak aloud. Trust was the foundation of MNA society. The idea that someone at the highest levels had betrayed that trust, was actively working to destroy everything they had built...

"I will be careful," Aiyana said. "And I will find them. Whoever did this to you, whoever is feeding our enemies the means to hurt us, I will find them."

"I believe you." Kele released her arm and sank back against his pillows, exhaustion suddenly visible in every line of his face. "I believe you will. I only hope you find them before they do more damage."

* * *

Renna was waiting for her in the corridor outside Kele's room.

She looked better than she had the last time they spoke, some color returned to her cheeks, some steadiness to her posture. But her eyes still held the watchfulness of someone who had learned that safety was an illusion, that danger could wear any face.

"He talked to you," Renna said. It was not a question.

"He talked to me."

"Did he tell you about the traitor?"

Aiyana nodded. "He confirmed what you suspected. Someone with high-level access has been feeding information to the Quiet Choir."

"Not just someone." Renna glanced down the corridor, checking for listeners, then lowered her voice. "I have been thinking about this every day since I returned. Going over everything I heard in the facility, everything the guards said when they thought I could not hear. And I think I know how to narrow the search."

"How?"

"The extraction. Our extraction." Renna's eyes met hers. "The codes were compromised, yes. But think about what else they knew. They knew when we would come. They knew our approach routes. They knew to expand the facility to contain more cells, as if they were expecting to capture more of us."

"That could have come from the compromised codes. From Elias's intelligence being intercepted."

"Some of it, yes. But not all of it." Renna shook her head. "The codes came from the underground network in Nova-Providence. The approach routes were planned here, in Wakana Station, after the Council approved the operation. The only way the Pale Cities could have known both is if someone had access to both sources of information."

Aiyana felt the logic clicking into place. "Someone who knew about Elias's intelligence and also knew about our operational planning."

"Someone on the Council," Renna said quietly. "Or someone close enough to the Council to have access to their discussions."

The accusation was staggering. The Rooted Council was the heart of MNA governance, the circle of elders and representatives who guided their society's decisions. To suggest that one of them was a traitor was to suggest that the rot had reached the very center of everything they believed in.

"You cannot make that accusation without proof," Aiyana said.

"I know. That is why I have not made it." Renna's voice was bitter. "That is why I told you, and only you. Because you are young enough not to be the traitor yourself, and because you have more reason than anyone to want to find the truth."

Aiyana thought about Speaks-Low, still in enemy hands.

About Talon and River-Runs-Deep, whose bodies had been buried three days ago. About Kele, broken in a room designed for breaking. All of it because someone had betrayed them. Someone who was supposed to protect them.

"What do you suggest?"

"The Elias extraction. It is still happening, yes?"

"I leave tomorrow night. Small team, eastern corridor approach."

"Who knows the details of the operation?"

Aiyana considered. "Chogan Grayfeather approved it. The Council was informed in general terms. My team knows the specifics. The network contacts who will guide Elias to the extraction point."

"Then we watch." Renna's eyes were hard. "If the operation is compromised, if the Pale Cities know you are coming, then the traitor had access to that information. We narrow the list of suspects. We pay attention to who knew what and when."

"And if the operation is not compromised? If I bring Elias back safely?"

"Then we keep watching. Keep testing. Feed different information through different channels and see which leaks reach the enemy." Renna's voice was cold, methodical. "The traitor will make a mistake eventually. They always do. We just have to be paying attention when it happens."

Aiyana looked at the woman before her, at the transformation that captivity and rescue had worked on someone who had once been, by all accounts, gentle and idealistic. The Renna who had been captured would not have spoken this way. The Renna who had returned was something harder, something forged in the fires of betrayal and survival.

"You have changed," Aiyana said quietly.

"We all change." Renna's expression softened slightly. "The question is whether we change into something that can still fight for what matters, or something that forgets why we were fighting in the first place." She touched Aiyana's arm briefly. "Come back safe. Bring Elias home. And when you return, we will find the traitor together."

She turned and walked away, her footsteps silent on the woven floors of the grandmother oak. Aiyana watched her go, then turned toward the stairs that led down to the station's operations center.

Tomorrow night. The extraction. Another mission into enemy territory, another chance for everything to go wrong.

But this time, she would be watching. Watching the operation, yes, but also watching the people around her. Looking for the signs that Renna and Kele had identified. Searching for the face of betrayal among faces she had been taught to trust.

Sitala was waiting for her at the base of the tree, the eagle's wing fully healed now, her golden feathers catching the late afternoon light. Through their bond, Aiyana felt her companion's readiness, the eagerness to fly again after days of recovery.

We hunt? Sitala asked in the wordless way of their communication.

We hunt, Aiyana replied. *For a man who needs saving. And for a traitor who needs finding.*

The eagle spread her wings and launched into the sky, circling upward on thermals that rose from the sun-warmed clearing. Aiyana watched her climb and felt something settle into place within her own chest. A purpose. A direction. A hunt that would not end until she had found what she was looking for.

The river of events was carrying them all toward something. A confrontation. A revelation. A moment when the quiet border would finally break and everything would change.

Aiyana did not know what that moment would look like. She knew only that she intended to be ready when it came.

She turned toward the operations center and began planning for the mission that would either bring her answers or bring her death.

Either way, the waiting was over.

The hunt had begun.

10

The Untethered

The signal should not have existed.

Aiyana had detected it while running final diagnostics on her sky-suit, preparing for the extraction mission that would launch at nightfall. A harmonic frequency threading through the Bioweb's background hum, so faint that she might have dismissed it as noise if she had not been listening with the particular attention that came from days of searching for anomalies.

But she had been listening. And the signal was not noise.

It was a beacon. Unauthorized. Emanating from somewhere in the mountain forests three days' travel east of Wakana Station, in territory that should have been empty of any technology capable of producing such a signature.

She should have reported it. Protocol demanded that any unexplained signals be logged and investigated through proper channels. But proper channels meant the Council, and Renna's words echoed in her mind: *If the traitor is highly placed, they may be in a position to intercept any report you make.*

So instead of reporting, Aiyana went looking.

The extraction team was not scheduled to depart until after dark. She had hours. And Sitala, fully recovered now, was eager to fly.

They left Wakana Station in the late morning, telling no one, following the thread of the signal through forests that grew denser and older as they traveled east. The Bioweb sang differently here, its harmonics deeper and more complex, resonating with trees that had been growing since before any human walked this land. Aiyana flew low, skimming the canopy, while Sitala ranged ahead, scouting the terrain with eyes that could spot movement from a thousand meters.

The signal grew stronger as they approached. And stranger.

It was not a standard MNA frequency. The harmonic pattern was different, experimental, as if someone had taken Bioweb principles and pushed them in directions the technology had never been designed to go. Aiyana felt it resonating with her sky-suit in ways that made her skin prickle, frequencies that danced at the edge of discomfort.

Sitala's warning came a moment before Aiyana would have flown directly into the clearing.

People below. Armed. They have seen us.

Aiyana pulled up sharply, banking into the cover of a massive oak whose branches spread wide enough to shield her from view. Through Sitala's eyes, she studied what lay below.

A compound. Not built in the MNA style of grown structures and organic integration, but not Pale City manufacture either. Something in between: modular buildings constructed from salvaged materials, surrounded by equipment she did not recognize, all of it humming with the strange frequencies that had led her here.

And people. A dozen that she could see, wearing clothing that mixed MNA and Pale City elements in deliberate defiance of both traditions. They moved with the alert efficiency of people who expected trouble and were prepared to meet it.

"You can come down." The voice came from below, amplified by some device Aiyana could not see. "We know you are there. We have been watching you for the past ten minutes."

Aiyana considered her options. Flight was possible; her sky-suit could outpace most pursuers. But these people had technology she did not understand, and running would leave her questions unanswered.

She descended.

* * *

The woman waiting for her at the edge of the clearing was tall and lean, with the weathered features of someone who had spent years working outdoors.

She wore a sky-suit, but it was unlike any Aiyana had seen: modified, augmented, bristling with additions that looked more like weapons than tools. Her hair was cut short in the practical style of engineers, and her eyes held the particular intensity of someone who had long ago stopped caring what others thought of her choices.

"Aiyana Waketah," the woman said. "The hero of the detention facility extraction. Or the failure, depending on whom you ask."

"You know who I am."

"We know everyone worth knowing." The woman gestured toward the compound behind her. "I am Tavani. This is our home. Or our laboratory. Or our armory. The distinction depends on the day."

"Who are you?"

"We are the people the Rooted Council pretends do not exist."

Tavani began walking toward the compound, clearly expecting Aiyana to follow. "We are the engineers who asked questions the Council did not want answered. The researchers who pursued lines of inquiry that were deemed too dangerous or too aggressive. The believers who looked at the Pale Cities' weapons and decided that the MNA needed weapons of its own."

Aiyana followed, her senses alert for threats, Sitala circling overhead. "The Untethered."

Tavani glanced back, a hint of surprise in her expression. "You have heard of us."

"Rumors. Whispers about rogue technologists who rejected the Council's limits." Aiyana studied the compound as they approached, noting the defensive positions, the sensor arrays, the equipment whose purpose she could not guess. "I thought you were a myth."

"Myths do not build resonance weapons." Tavani stopped at the entrance to the largest structure, a building that hummed with contained power. "Myths do not develop countermeasures to the Nullwave. Myths do not spend fifteen years preparing for the war the Council insists will never come."

"The Council works to prevent war."

"The Council works to maintain the illusion that war can be prevented." Tavani's voice hardened. "But war is coming, Aiyana Waketah. It has been coming since the Pale Cities decided that our existence was an obstacle to their expansion. The only question is whether we will be prepared when it arrives, or whether we will be slaughtered while still insisting that negotiation is possible."

She opened the door and led Aiyana inside.

The interior of the building was a workshop, a laboratory,

and an arsenal all at once. Tables covered with half-assembled devices. Screens displaying schematics that Aiyana recognized as Bioweb architecture, modified in ways she had never imagined. And weapons. Racks of them, along the walls, some familiar in their basic design, others completely alien.

"This is what we do," Tavani said. "We take the principles the Council has deemed too dangerous to explore and we explore them anyway. We build the tools our people will need when the Pale Cities finally decide to destroy us."

Aiyana moved through the space, her engineer's eye cataloging what she saw. Harmonic disruptors, designed to interfere with Pale City electronics. Shield generators that could deflect the frequencies the Nullwave used. And something else, something larger, occupying an entire section of the building, covered in sensor arrays and power conduits.

"What is that?"

Tavani moved to stand beside the device, her hand resting on its surface with something like affection. "This is a resonance amplifier. It takes the frequencies of the Bioweb and magnifies them a thousandfold." She met Aiyana's eyes. "With this, we could reach into Nova-Providence itself. We could shut down their power grid, disable their vehicles, blind their surveillance systems. We could bring the Pale Cities to their knees without firing a single conventional weapon."

"That would kill people."

"It would kill fewer people than the war the Quiet Choir is planning." Tavani's voice was patient, as if explaining something obvious to a slow student. "The Nullwave they are developing will devastate our eastern territories. Thousands will die in the initial strike. Thousands more in the aftermath, when the systems they depend on collapse. And the Council's response? Negotiation. Diplomacy. Words that the Pale Cities interpret as weakness."

"So your solution is to become what they are. To build weapons of mass destruction and call it defense."

"My solution is to survive." Tavani stepped closer, her intensity radiating like heat. "The Pale Cities do not care about our philosophy. They do not care about balance or harmony or the relationship between humans and the land. They care about power. About control. About eliminating anything that threatens their way of life. And we threaten them, Aiyana. By existing, by thriving, by proving that their way is not the only way, we threaten everything they believe. They will destroy us if they can. The only way to prevent that is to make the cost of trying too high."

Aiyana thought about Kele, broken by Pale City interrogators. About Speaks-Low, still in enemy hands. About the Nullwave, ready for deployment, aimed at everything her people had built.

She thought about the traitor, somewhere in the MNA's highest councils, feeding information to the enemy.

"Why are you showing me this?" she asked.

"Because you are not like the others." Tavani moved to a table where a map of MNA territory was displayed, marked with symbols Aiyana did not recognize. "You have seen what the Pale Cities do. You have lost people to their cruelty. You know, in your bones, that the Council's faith in negotiation is misplaced."

"You do not know what I believe."

"I know what you have done." Tavani tapped the map at a point Aiyana recognized as the location of the detention facility. "I know you went into enemy territory against orders. I know you risked everything to save your people. I know you made choices the Council would never have approved, because the Council does not understand what it means to fight."

"The extraction was authorized."

"The extraction was sanitized. Wrapped in diplomatic justifications that made it palatable to the moderates. But you and I both know what it really was: an act of war. A statement that the MNA will not abandon its people to enemy cells." Tavani's eyes burned with conviction. "That is the kind of thinking we need. That is the kind of person who should be making decisions, not the elders who have forgotten what it means to be in danger."

Aiyana felt the pull of Tavani's words, the seductive logic that promised simple solutions to complex problems. Strike first. Strike hard. Make them fear to attack.

But she had seen what that logic produced in the Pale Cities. She had seen the detention facilities, the propaganda, the systematic dehumanization of everyone who did not fit the approved narrative. She had seen what happened when a society decided that survival justified anything.

"I understand what you are offering," she said carefully. "And I understand why you believe it is necessary. But I am not here to join you."

"Then why are you here?"

"I followed a signal. I wanted to know what it was." Aiyana met Tavani's gaze steadily. "Now I know. And I have a decision to make about what to do with that knowledge."

Tavani studied her for a long moment. Something shifted in her expression, a recalculation, a reassessment.

"You could report us. Tell the Council where we are. They would send Guardians to shut us down, confiscate our research, probably put us on trial for unauthorized development of restricted technologies." She did not sound concerned. "But you will not do that."

"How do you know?"

"Because you came alone. Because you did not report the signal before investigating. Because you are already keeping secrets from the people who are supposed to trust you." Tavani smiled, the expression sharp and knowing. "You suspect there is a traitor in the Council. Someone feeding information to the Pale Cities. You do not know whom you can trust, so you trust no one. That makes you more like us than you want to admit."

The accuracy of the observation was unsettling. Aiyana had not spoken of her suspicions to anyone except Renna, had not shared Kele's warnings with a single soul. Yet Tavani knew.

"How did you know about the traitor?"

"We have been watching the Council for years. We have noticed patterns. Operations that were compromised. Intelligence that reached the Pale Cities before it should have. We do not know who the traitor is, but we know they exist." Tavani's voice hardened. "We have been trying to identify them. So far, we have failed. But we are closer than the Council's own security services, because we are not blinded by the assumption that everyone in power can be trusted."

"If you know there is a traitor, why have you not reported it?"

"Report it to whom? The Council that may include the traitor? The security services that answer to the Council?" Tavani shook her head. "We survive by staying hidden. By watching without being watched. If we revealed what we know, we would reveal ourselves. And then we would be silenced before we could help."

Aiyana stood in the workshop, surrounded by weapons

that could devastate cities and technology that pushed the boundaries of everything the MNA believed, and tried to reconcile what she was hearing with what she had been taught to believe.

The Untethered were dangerous. Their philosophy led to escalation, to an arms race that could consume both societies. Everything she had learned about balance and restraint argued against their approach.

But they were also right about the traitor. Right about the Council's blindness. Right that the Nullwave was coming and that negotiation alone would not stop it.

"I will not join you," she said finally. "And I will not report you. Not yet. Not until I understand more about what is happening."

"That is all we ask." Tavani extended her hand. "An open mind. A willingness to see what others refuse to see. When the time comes, when the Council's failures become undeniable, you know where to find us."

Aiyana did not take the hand. But she did not refuse it either. She simply turned and walked out of the workshop, into the afternoon light, where Sitala was waiting.

The flight back to Wakana Station was silent. Aiyana needed time to process what she had learned, to fit this new piece into the puzzle she was assembling. The Untethered. The traitor. The Nullwave. The extraction that awaited her at nightfall.

She had left seeking answers. She had found only more questions.

But one thing had become clear: the MNA was not the unified society she had been taught to believe in. Beneath the surface of consensus and harmony, factions struggled for influence, secrets festered, and people made choices that the official narrative could not contain.

The Cold War was not just between the MNA and the Pale Cities. It was inside the MNA as well, a struggle over what kind of society they would become, what methods they would embrace, what lines they would cross in the name of survival.

Aiyana landed at Wakana Station as the sun began to set. Her team was assembling for the extraction. Elias was waiting to be saved. The mission demanded her focus.

She set aside thoughts of the Untethered and their weapons, their warnings, their offer of alliance. There would be time to deal with that later.

For now, there was work to do.

And somewhere in the darkness ahead, a young man who had risked everything for truth was running out of time.

11

The Long Walk

Elias had never realized how much of his life had been spent in artificial light.

The tunnels beneath Nova-Providence stretched for kilometers, a network of maintenance corridors and abandoned transit lines that the underground had converted into escape routes. He had been walking for two days now, guided by people whose faces he never saw clearly in the dim emergency lighting, sleeping in alcoves that smelled of rust and stagnant water, eating food that tasted of nothing but survival.

Above him, somewhere in the impossible distance of the surface, the city continued its eternal hum. The Signal Mesh broadcast its reassurances. Citizens went about their lives, believing what they had been taught to believe. And the Doctrine Keepers searched for him with an intensity that had forced the underground to scatter, to abandon safe houses, to push him deeper into passages that had not been used in years.

Mira walked beside him, her footsteps silent on the corroded metal of the tunnel floor. She had not left his side since the night the raids began, guiding him through a city he thought he knew but had never truly seen. The Nova-Providence that existed in the underground was a different place entirely: a shadow city of hidden rooms and secret passages, of people who had learned to be invisible because visibility meant death.

"We are close," she said. Her voice was barely above a whisper, though they had not encountered another soul in hours. "Another day, perhaps two. Then we reach the eastern corridor."

"And then?"

"Then we wait. The MNA will send someone to bring you across." She glanced at him, her expression unreadable in the half-light. "Assuming they still want you."

"Why would they not want me?"

"Because your intelligence led to a trap. People died, Elias. MNA operatives died because of information you provided." Her voice carried no accusation, only fact. "Some will blame you for that. Some will wonder if you were part of the trap."

The words landed like stones in his chest. He had heard about the failed extraction, the deaths, the capture of a senior commander. He had not known that his intelligence had contributed to it.

"I did not know," he said. "The codes were genuine when I received them. Someone must have compromised them afterward."

"I believe you." Mira's hand touched his arm briefly, a gesture of reassurance. "But belief is not proof. You will have to convince them yourself, when you reach the other side."

They walked in silence for a while. The tunnel curved gradually, following the contours of some ancient infrastructure that Elias could not identify. Pipes ran along the ceiling, their surfaces thick with mineral deposits. The air grew cooler as they descended, carrying the smell of deep earth and forgotten spaces.

"Why do you do this?" he asked finally. "Risk your life to help people escape?"

Mira was quiet for a long moment. When she spoke, her voice was softer than he had heard it before.

"My mother was a teacher. Before the current regime, before the Doctrine Keepers had full control over education. She taught history. Real history, not the version they tell now." Mira's footsteps did not falter, but something in her posture had changed. "When they started rewriting the curriculum, she refused to teach the lies. She said that a society built on falsehood could not stand, that truth was more important than comfort."

"What happened to her?"

"She disappeared. One night she was there, and the next morning she was gone. No arrest, no trial, no explanation. Just absence." Mira's voice hardened. "I was twelve. I spent years believing she had abandoned me, because that was easier than believing the alternative. It was not until I found the underground that I learned the truth about what happens to people who refuse to lie."

"I am sorry."

"Do not be sorry. Be useful." She turned to face him, and in the dim light he could see the fierce determination in her eyes. "You have information. Things you learned in the Cultural Ministry, things you read in the archives before they were sealed. That information can help people understand what their government really is. That is why we are getting you out. Not because of your codes or your intelligence about facilities. Because you know things that can change how people think."

Elias thought about the book he had been reading when the raids began. The true history of the Long March, of the choice that had been made generations ago, of the lies that had been constructed to justify that choice. He thought about the archives he had accessed in his official capacity, the documents that told a different story than the one broadcast on the Signal Mesh.

"I do know things," he said slowly. "But I do not know if anyone wants to hear them. People believe what they believe because it is easier. Changing that..."

"Changing that is the only thing that matters." Mira began walking again, and he followed. "The Nullwave cannot destroy the MNA. Even if they deploy it, even if they devastate entire regions, the Alliance will survive and rebuild. But if we can change how our own people think, if we can break the hold the Doctrine Keepers have on what citizens believe, then everything changes. The whole foundation of this conflict shifts."

"You really believe that?"

"I have to believe something." Her voice carried a weariness that belied her years. "Otherwise, what is the point of any of this?"

* * *

They slept in shifts in a maintenance alcove, their backs against pipes that had not carried water in decades.

Elias dreamed of his family. His mother's face, disappointed but unsurprised when he told her he was leaving the Cultural Ministry. His father's silence, which had always been harder to bear than anger. His sister, who had stopped speaking to him after he began asking questions that made her uncomfortable.

In the dream, they stood in the apartment where he had

grown up, surrounded by the carefully curated decorations that proclaimed their loyalty to the Pale Cities' ideals. His mother held a photograph of him as a child, her fingers tracing the frame.

"You were such a good boy," she said. "You believed everything we taught you."

"I still believe in truth," dream-Elias replied. "Is that not what you taught me?"

"We taught you to survive." His father's voice, speaking for the first time in years. "Truth is not the same as survival. Sometimes they are opposites."

He woke to Mira's hand on his shoulder, her face close to his in the darkness.

"Someone is coming," she breathed. "Stay quiet."

They pressed themselves into the shadows of the alcove, barely breathing. Footsteps echoed in the tunnel, the sound bouncing off the curved walls in ways that made it impossible to judge distance or direction. Light flickered in the distance, the beam of a handheld lamp sweeping across the passage.

"Patrol," Mira whispered. "They should not be this deep. Something has changed."

The footsteps grew closer. Elias could hear voices now, too indistinct to make out words but carrying the tone of men who were tired and irritated and wished they were somewhere else. Routine patrol, not a targeted search. At least, he hoped so.

The light swept past their alcove without pausing. The footsteps continued, fading into the distance, taking the voices with them. Mira did not move for a long time after the sound had completely disappeared.

"They are extending their search patterns," she said finally. "The Doctrine Keepers must have pressured the civil authority to increase tunnel security." She stood, gathering the small pack that held their supplies. "We need to move faster. If they are patrolling this deep, the routes we planned may be compromised."

"Is there another way?"

"There is always another way." Mira consulted something in her pack, a map or a device that Elias could not see clearly. "But the other ways are more dangerous. Less traveled, less maintained. Parts of them have not been used since before I was born."

"And if we stay on the planned route?"

"We risk walking into a patrol that is not tired and irritated. One that is looking specifically for us." She met his eyes. "Your face has been on the Signal Mesh for three days now. *Traitor to the Renewal. Agent of the savage alliance. Danger to all loyal citizens.* They are offering a reward for information leading to your capture. A significant one."

Elias felt the weight of that settle over him. He had known he was being hunted, but hearing the specifics made it real in a way that abstract knowledge could not.

"Then we take the other way," he said.

Mira nodded and led him deeper into the tunnels.

* * *

The older passages were different.

The infrastructure here dated from before the current city had been built, from an era when the Pale Cities had been smaller, more desperate, still struggling to establish themselves in the shadow of MNA prosperity. The walls were rough-hewn stone rather than processed metal, the ceilings low enough that Elias had to duck in places. Water seeped through cracks, forming pools that reflected their lamp light in unexpected ways.

And there were signs of habitation. Old ones, faded, but unmistakable. Names carved into walls. Dates that stretched back generations. Symbols that Elias did not recognize but that clearly meant something to whoever had made them.

"Who lived here?" he asked.

"The ones who did not fit." Mira ran her fingers over a carved name, her expression distant. "Before the Doctrine Keepers consolidated control, there were people who resisted. Who remembered the truth about the Long March, who refused to accept the official narrative. They were pushed out of public life, denied employment, cut off from the systems that made survival possible in the cities."

"What happened to them?"

"Some fled to the frontier. Some tried to cross into MNA territory." She continued walking, her lamp casting long shadows. "Some came down here. Built communities in the spaces the city had forgotten. Lived for years, sometimes generations, outside the system."

"And now?"

"Now they are gone. The last of the old communities dispersed decades ago. The Doctrine Keepers found most of them eventually. The rest..." She shrugged. "Died out. Lost hope. Joined the underground network and lost their separate identity."

Elias thought about the people who had carved their names into these walls. People who had lived their entire lives in hiding, who had raised children in darkness, who had clung to truths that the surface world wanted to forget. They were his predecessors, he realized. The first generation of those who chose truth over survival.

Most of them had not survived. That was the lesson the walls taught, if he was willing to learn it.

"Why did they stay?" he asked. "If they could have fled to MNA territory, why remain here?"

"Because this was their home." Mira's voice was soft. "Because they believed they could change things from within. Because they had families, communities, lives that they could not simply abandon." She glanced back at him. "The same reasons most people stay in places that hurt them. Love. Hope. The inability to imagine themselves anywhere else."

"And you? Why do you stay?"

"I stay because someone has to." She stopped at a junction where the passage split into three directions, consulting her map again. "If everyone who sees the truth leaves, then only the believers remain. The lies become more powerful, not less. The system perpetuates itself because no one is left to challenge it."

"But you help people like me escape."

"I help people whose truth is more useful on the other side." She chose the middle passage and began walking. "You have information that can be broadcast back, that can reach people through channels the Doctrine Keepers cannot control. Your escape is not abandonment. It is strategy."

Elias followed her into the darkness, turning her words over in his mind. Strategy. He had never thought of himself as strategic. He had simply been a man who read the wrong books, asked the wrong questions, and found himself unable to un-know what he had learned.

But Mira was right about one thing. The information he carried could matter. The archives he had accessed, the documents he had read, the patterns he had noticed in the gaps between official records. All of it pointed to a truth that the Doctrine Keepers had spent generations burying: the Pale Cities were not victims. They were descendants of people who had chosen extraction over integration, who had rejected the opportunity to live in balance because balance required compromise.

That truth, broadcast widely enough, could shake the foundations of everything his people believed about themselves.

Whether they would listen was another question. Whether truth could compete with comfortable lies in the minds of people who had been raised on those lies from birth.

But he would try. That was all anyone could do.

Try, and hope that trying was enough.

* * *

On the third day, they reached the edge.

The tunnel ended at a metal door, rusted but still solid, set into a wall of ancient stone. Beyond it, Mira said, lay the eastern corridor: a strip of abandoned territory between the outer reaches of Nova-Providence's influence and the beginning of MNA-monitored land. A no-man's-zone where neither side maintained permanent presence, where the rules of both societies gave way to something older and simpler.

"This is where I leave you," Mira said.

Elias turned to face her. In the three days they had traveled together, she had become the closest thing he had to a friend. She had kept him alive, kept him moving, kept him believing that the other side was worth reaching.

"Come with me," he said.

"I cannot." Her smile was sad but certain. "My work is here. My people are here. The ones who cannot run, who have to stay and fight in whatever small ways they can." She pressed something into his hand: a data chip, small enough to hide almost anywhere. "Everything I know about the underground network. Contacts, safe houses, communication methods. Give it to the MNA. Maybe they can use it to help more people escape."

"Mira..."

"Do not make this harder than it needs to be." She stepped back, her expression composed. "Through this door, follow the corridor east until you see the old watchtower. Wait there. Someone will come for you before dawn."

"How will they know where to find me?"

"They know." She turned toward the darkness of the tunnel, the way back to the city that had made her and broken her and given her purpose all at once. "Survive, Elias Harren. Make the truth matter. That is how you repay the debt you owe."

Then she was gone, her footsteps fading into the distance, leaving him alone at the edge of everything he had ever known.

Elias stood in the darkness for a long time. Then he opened the door and stepped through into the night air of the eastern corridor, where the stars burned overhead with an intensity he had never seen through Nova-Providence's filtered sky.

The watchtower was a shadow against the horizon. He began walking toward it, one foot in front of the other, carrying his truth toward people who might or might not want to hear it.

Behind him, the door closed with a sound like finality.

Ahead, the border waited.

And somewhere in the darkness between, the people who would decide his fate were already moving to meet him.

12

The Crossing

The watchtower was a ruin of stone and rusted metal, barely visible against the pre-dawn sky.

Aiyana approached from the west, her sky-suit's harmonics dampened to near-silence, Sitala ranging ahead to scout the terrain. The eastern corridor stretched around them: a wasteland of abandoned structures and overgrown roads, the detritus of a border that had been contested and redrawn a dozen times over the past century. Nothing moved in the gray light except wind through dead grass and the distant shapes of animals who had learned that this place belonged to no one.

Her team was small. Catches-The-Wind flew parallel to her position, a shadow against the clouds. On the ground, two Guardians moved through the scrubland: Naya, whose skill with harmonic disruption had saved them twice during the last extraction, and Kohen, a tracker who could read terrain the way others read text. Four people to retrieve one defector. Four people who might be walking into another trap.

Aiyana had told no one about her visit to the Untethered. She had not shared what Tavani had shown her, what she had learned about the weapons being developed in hidden laboratories. That knowledge sat in her chest like a stone, another secret among the secrets she was accumulating.

But she had taken precautions. The extraction route she had filed with operations was not the route they were actually taking. The timing she had reported was off by two hours. If this mission was compromised, if the traitor had access to her plans, the enemy would be waiting in the wrong place at the wrong time.

It was a test. And she hated that it had to be.

Movement at the tower, Sitala reported. *One figure. Human. Alone.*

Aiyana signaled the team to hold position and descended toward the watchtower, landing on a section of collapsed wall that gave her elevation and cover. Through the pre-dawn murk, she could see the figure Sitala had spotted: a man standing in the tower's entrance, looking westward with the posture of someone who had been waiting a long time.

Elias Harren. She knew him before Sitala confirmed it, knew him by the way he stood, by the particular set of his shoulders that she remembered from a drainage tunnel beneath Nova-Providence. He looked worse than when she had left him. Thinner. Older than his years. The clothes he wore were stained with tunnel grime and exhaustion, and she could see even from this distance that the weeks since their escape had cost him more than she had imagined.

He was alive. After everything, after the trap that his codes had sprung, after the silence that had followed his last transmission, he was alive. She had not realized how much she had feared otherwise until the relief washed through her.

She dropped from the wall, landing softly on the rubble-strewn ground, and walked toward him with her hands visible. Non-threatening, but ready to move if this was a deception. She wanted to believe he was still the man who had pressed a data chip into her palm and told her to *make it matter*. But wanting was not the same as knowing, and the codes he had provided had nearly gotten her team killed.

"Elias," she said.

He turned toward her voice, and she saw the moment when hope and fear warred across his features. Hope that rescue had arrived. Fear that it might be something else. Then recognition, and something that looked almost like wonder.

"Aiyana." Her name in his voice, rough with disuse. "You came yourself."

"I told you to stay alive." She stopped three meters away, maintaining distance. "You look like you barely managed it."

"It was a near thing." He tried to smile, but it did not reach his eyes. "After you escaped, the Doctrine Keepers came down hard. The network that helped me reach you was compromised. People died. People I had brought into danger." His voice cracked. "And the codes I gave you..."

"We need to talk about those." Aiyana kept her tone level, though something in her chest tightened. "I am here to bring you across. But first, I need to know something."

"Anything."

"The facility codes. The ones you provided for the detention facility extraction. Were they genuine when you sent them?"

Pain flickered across his face, followed by something harder. "They were genuine. I obtained them from a source I trusted, someone who had access to facility security protocols. I do not know how they were compromised, but I swear to you, they were real when I sent them."

"People died because of those codes."

"I know." His voice cracked. "Mira told me. The woman who guided me through the tunnels. She said your people would blame me, and I understand why. But I did not betray you, Aiyana. Someone else did that. Someone intercepted my intelligence and fed you false information using my name."

Aiyana studied him, looking for the signs of deception she had been trained to recognize. Micro-expressions. Inconsistencies in posture. The subtle tells that revealed when someone was constructing a narrative rather than recounting truth.

She saw exhaustion. She saw grief. She saw the particular devastation of someone who had burned his entire life to the ground and was only now beginning to feel the heat.

What she did not see was guilt. Not the guilt of a betrayer, at least. Only the guilt of someone who had been part of a disaster without understanding how.

She remembered his hand in hers in that drainage tunnel. The warmth of his fingers. The way he had said *I'll try* when she told him to stay alive. Whatever else had happened, whatever deceptions had been woven around him, that moment had been real.

"All right," she said. "We move now. Stay close to me, do exactly what I tell you, and we might all survive this."

"Thank you." The words came out rough with emotion. "I did not know if anyone would come. After the codes failed, after everything fell apart, I thought maybe..."

"Someone always comes." She activated her comm link, signaling the team. "That is what we do."

* * *

They moved west through the corridor, the sky brightening toward a dawn that would make them visible to anyone watching.

Aiyana kept Elias between herself and Catches-The-Wind, with Naya and Kohen flanking on the ground. The formation was defensive, designed to protect the asset while maintaining flexibility to respond to threats. Standard extraction protocol, drilled into her during months of Guardian training.

But nothing about this felt standard.

Elias moved with the awkwardness of someone unused to physical exertion, his footsteps heavy on the uneven ground. He stumbled twice in the first kilometer, and Aiyana had to slow her pace to match his. A city dweller, she thought. A man of books and archives, not open terrain. But he kept moving, kept pushing himself forward with a determination that reminded her why she had trusted him in the first place.

"The Cultural Ministry," she said, keeping her voice low. Conversation would help him focus, keep him from freezing if danger came. "You told me you found things in the archives. Inconsistencies."

"I found more after you left." He kept his eyes on the ground, watching for obstacles. "Documents that should have been destroyed generations ago. Records of the original agreements between your people and the first colonists. Treaties that were signed and then erased from history." He glanced at her. "The Doctrine Keepers are thorough, but history is vast. They cannot edit everything. If you look carefully enough, you can see where the fabric has been cut and re-stitched."

"And when you saw it?"

"I started looking for more. Found books that should not have survived the censors. Accessed archives that were supposed to be restricted. The more I looked, the more I found, until the picture became clear." His voice carried the weight of revelation. "Everything my people believe about themselves, about the MNA, about why we live the way we do. It is all constructed. All of it."

"You told me something like that before," Aiyana said. "In the tunnel. You said your father had died trying to find the truth."

"I remember." He touched his chest, where she knew he kept his father's compass. "I have been carrying his work with me. Finishing what he started." A bitter laugh. "He would have been proud, I think. And terrified. The truth is more dangerous than either of us imagined."

"What will you do with what you know?" she asked.

"Tell people. Anyone who will listen." He stumbled again, caught himself. "The underground believes that truth can change minds. That if enough people hear what really happened, what is really happening, the system will lose its hold." He looked at her. "Do you believe that?"

Aiyana thought about the question. About the propaganda she had seen, the depth of belief it produced, the generations of people who had been raised on lies and knew no other foundation.

"I believe truth matters," she said carefully. "But I do not know if it is enough. People believe what they need to believe. Changing that takes more than information."

"Then what does it take?"

"I do not know. If I did, maybe we would not be here." She signaled the team to slow as they approached a rise that would expose them against the lightening sky. "But trying is better than surrendering. Even if we fail, at least we tried."

Elias was quiet for a moment. Then: "You sound like Mira."

"Tell me about her."

"The woman who brought me through the tunnels. She stayed behind. Said her work was there, helping others escape." His voice caught. "She gave me everything she knew about the underground network. Said to give it to you."

He reached into his pocket and produced a small data chip, holding it out to Aiyana. She took it, feeling the weight of trust it represented. A woman she would never meet had given a stranger her secrets, betting everything on the hope that those secrets would be used well.

"I will make sure it reaches the right people," Aiyana said.

"Thank you." Elias's voice was barely a whisper. "She deserves that. They all do."

* * *

The attack came as the sun breached the horizon.

Sitala's warning arrived a heartbeat before the first shot, a pulse of alarm through their bond that sent Aiyana diving sideways, pulling Elias with her. The projectile passed through the space where they had been standing, a needle of compressed air that would have dropped them both.

"Contact!" Naya's voice crackled over the comm. "Multiple hostiles, eastern ridge!"

Aiyana rolled to her feet, dragging Elias into the cover of a collapsed wall. Her mind was already calculating: enemy position, team disposition, distance to the border. They were close. So close. Another two kilometers and they would be in MNA-monitored territory, where pursuit would be intercepted.

"How many?" she demanded.

"Six, maybe eight." Kohen's voice was calm, professional. "Light patrol, not a full intercept team. They were waiting, but not in force."

Waiting. They had known the extraction was happening. But

they had expected the wrong time, the wrong route. The force they had positioned was designed for a smaller window, not the actual approach.

The test had worked. Someone had leaked the false information, and the enemy had acted on it.

Which meant the traitor was real. And they had access to Guardian operations.

Aiyana filed the revelation away for later. Right now, survival took priority.

"Naya, disruption pattern delta. Kohen, find us a path. Catches-The-Wind, keep them off our backs." She gripped Elias's arm. "Stay low, stay close, move when I move."

"I understand." His voice was steady despite the fear in his eyes. Whatever else he was, he was not a coward.

Naya's harmonic disruptor activated with a sound like singing glass, frequencies cascading outward in patterns designed to scramble electronics and disorient anyone relying on enhanced senses. The enemy fire faltered, shots going wide as their targeting systems struggled against the interference.

"Move!" Aiyana surged forward, pulling Elias with her, using the disruption window to cover ground. Kohen led them through a gully that provided natural cover, his tracker's instincts finding the path of least exposure.

Behind them, Catches-The-Wind engaged. Aiyana heard the distinctive hum of his sky-suit's offensive systems, the crack of return fire, the shouts of men who had expected an easy interception and were discovering their mistake.

A kilometer. Half a kilometer. The terrain was changing, the abandoned structures giving way to open ground that marked the true border. MNA sensors would be tracking them now. If they could reach the perimeter, reinforcements would arrive.

"Almost there," Kohen reported. "Three hundred meters to the line."

Elias was flagging, his breath coming in ragged gasps, his pace slowing despite his best efforts. Three days of tunnel travel followed by a running firefight had pushed him past his limits. Aiyana grabbed his arm and half-dragged him forward, willing strength into his failing legs.

"Come on. Just a little further."

"I am trying." He stumbled, nearly fell, caught himself. "I am sorry. I am not built for this."

"You do not have to be built for it. You just have to survive it."

They crossed the line.

Aiyana felt the shift in the Bioweb's harmonics, the subtle change that marked the transition from contested territory to MNA-monitored space. Behind them, the pursuit faltered. The Pale City patrol would not follow across the line, not in daylight, not without risking an international incident that their superiors had not authorized.

"We are across," she said into her comm. "All units, confirm status."

"Catches-The-Wind, intact. Disengaging now."

"Naya, intact. Minor equipment damage."

"Kohen, intact. Path is clear ahead."

Aiyana let out a breath she had not realized she was holding. They had done it. Against compromised intelligence, against an enemy who had known they were coming, against the odds that seemed to stack higher with every mission.

Elias collapsed to his knees on MNA soil, his body finally surrendering to exhaustion. His hands pressed into the earth, and Aiyana saw tears cutting tracks through the dirt on his face.

"I made it," he whispered. "I actually made it."

"You made it." She crouched beside him, allowing herself a moment of shared relief. "You kept your promise."

He looked up at her, his eyes red with tears and dust and three days of fear. "You came back for me. After everything. After the codes failed and people died. You still came."

"You gave me the first real lead on my brother." Aiyana's voice was quieter than she intended. "You risked everything to help us escape Nova-Providence. Whatever happened with those codes, it was not your betrayal. I knew that the moment I saw you standing in that tower."

Elias reached into his shirt and pulled out his father's compass, the brass surface dull with wear. "He would have wanted me to cross. To see this." He looked at the MNA sky, at the colors that the Pale Cities' filtered atmosphere would never allow. "To know that another way of living was possible."

"Welcome to the Many Nations Alliance, Elias Harren." Aiyana helped him to his feet as the rest of the team gathered around them. "I hope the truth you carry was worth the journey."

"It will be," he said. "I will make it worth it."

The sun was fully up now, painting the sky in shades that reminded her of the observation deck at Wakana Station, of mornings watching the light change over the valley with her mother. Birds sang in the distance, their voices carrying on air that smelled of grass and growing things.

They had won this round. Elias was safe. The mission was complete.

But the traitor was still out there, feeding information to the enemy, waiting for the next opportunity to strike. And the

Nullwave was still being prepared, aimed at everything Aiyana had sworn to protect.

This was not an ending. It was barely a beginning.

She led her team and their asset westward, toward Wakana Station, toward the debriefings and decisions that awaited. And in her pocket, Mira's data chip waited to reveal its secrets. Another weapon in a war that was only just beginning to show its true shape.

13

The Sound of Breaking

The Quiet Choir arrived at the secondary facility three hours before dawn.

Lucian watched them from his post at the security checkpoint, his face carefully neutral as two unmarked vehicles passed through the gates. The vehicles were standard government transport, unremarkable in every way, but the passengers they carried were anything but. He recognized the lead figure as she stepped out: Dr. Seren Volk, the Choir's chief interrogation specialist, a woman whose reputation preceded her like a cold wind.

She was small, almost delicate, with gray hair pulled back in a severe knot and eyes that seemed to catalog everything they touched. Nothing about her appearance suggested threat. That was what made her so effective. People expected monsters to look like monsters. Volk looked like someone's grandmother.

"Captain Ford." Her voice was soft, pleasant. "I understand you are the senior officer on site."

"I am." Lucian kept his posture correct, his tone professional. Nothing that could be interpreted as resistance or enthusiasm.

"We were not informed of your arrival."

"The Prime Councillor's authorization came through an hour ago. Emergency protocols." She produced a data tablet, displaying orders that bore Halding's electronic signature. "The MNA prisoner is to be transferred to Choir custody for specialized interrogation. Your facility will provide support as needed."

Lucian studied the orders, looking for any irregularity, any grounds on which he might delay. The authorization was legitimate. The signatures were valid. Whatever internal struggle had been happening in the capital, whatever resistance Halding and others had mounted against the Choir's demands, it was over.

The Choir had won.

"I will have my people prepare the prisoner for transfer," he said.

"That will not be necessary." Volk's smile did not reach her eyes. "The interrogation will take place here. Your facility has the infrastructure we require, and transport at this stage would be... counterproductive. The subject is more cooperative when kept in familiar surroundings."

Subject. Not prisoner. Not even a name. Lucian felt something cold settle in his stomach.

"The lower level has been prepared according to specifications," he said. "My people will show you the way."

"Your people will remain at their posts. The Choir's own security team will handle the subject." Volk gestured, and figures began emerging from the second vehicle: men and women in unmarked uniforms, carrying cases of equipment that Lucian did not want to think about. "We require complete operational isolation. No facility personnel in the lower level until we have concluded our work."

"Understood."

Volk studied him for a moment, her gaze sharp and assessing. "You seem troubled, Captain."

"I serve the Renewal." The words came automatically, the response drilled into every officer. "My personal feelings are irrelevant."

"Spoken like a true believer." Her smile widened slightly. "Or like a man who knows what answers are expected." She turned toward the facility entrance, her team falling in behind her. "We will require several days. Perhaps a week. When we are finished, you will have a subject ready to tell you anything you wish to know about MNA operations. The cost of that knowledge is not your concern."

She walked away, and Lucian stood at his post and watched the Choir disappear into the facility he was supposed to command.

* * *

The sounds began six hours later.

Lucian heard them from his office, two floors above the lower level, filtering through walls and floors that should have been soundproof. Not screams. Something worse. A keening that rose and fell in patterns that seemed almost musical, as if pain itself had been given voice and taught to sing.

He recognized the sound from intelligence briefings. The tuning devices that the Choir had developed, technologies that used harmonic frequencies to bypass the mind's defenses. They did not hurt the body. They did something worse: they hurt the self, the sense of coherence that held a person together.

Speaks-Low was down there. A man who had served his

people with distinction for decades. A man who had trained warriors and led missions and earned the respect of everyone who knew him. Now he was being unmade, one frequency at a time, his identity dissolved so that the Choir could extract what remained.

Lucian closed his eyes and listened to the sound of breaking.

He thought about his sister. About Lena, who had died at twelve because the frontier settlement where they lived did not have access to medicine that was common in the core cities. About the promise he had made at her grave, to serve something larger than himself, to make sure her death had meaning.

He had believed, once, that the Pale Cities represented that something larger. Progress. Order. A society that could provide for all its citizens, if only it had the resources to do so. He had believed that the MNA was hoarding those resources, keeping his people in poverty while they lived in harmony with a land they refused to share.

Now he knew better. Now he understood that the Pale Cities' poverty was self-inflicted, the result of systems designed to benefit the few at the expense of the many. Now he knew that the MNA had offered integration, had offered to share their knowledge and their land, and his ancestors had refused because integration meant giving up the right to take without asking.

The sound from below rose in pitch, then cut off abruptly. Silence, worse than the keening, because silence could mean anything.

Lucian opened his eyes and made a decision.

* * *

The dead drop was in a maintenance corridor on the facility's eastern wing.

A loose panel behind a ventilation unit, accessible only to someone who knew exactly where to look. Lucian had used it twice before: once to warn about the safe house raids, once to pass along information about the facility's security rotations. Each time, he had waited days for a response, never certain if his messages were reaching anyone, never knowing if the network he believed in actually existed.

Tonight, he did not have days.

He wrote quickly, encoding the message in the cipher the underground had taught him. *Choir has arrived. Tuning has begun. Subject will break within 48 hours. After that, all operational security is compromised. If extraction is planned, it must happen now.*

He added details: guard rotations, security codes, the layout of the lower level, everything he knew that might help someone planning a rescue. It was enough to earn him execution if discovered. It was not enough to guarantee success.

Nothing was ever enough. That was the nature of this work. You did what you could and hoped it mattered.

He sealed the message and placed it in the dead drop, then replaced the panel and walked back to his office as if nothing had happened.

The sounds from below had resumed. Different now. Quieter. The keening had become something closer to weeping, the resistance crumbling, the end approaching.

Lucian sat at his desk and pretended to review reports while a man he had never met was destroyed two floors beneath him.

* * *

Dawn came, and with it, a summons.

Dr. Volk's assistant appeared at Lucian's office door, a

young man with the blank expression of someone who had learned not to think about what his work required. "The doctor requests your presence in the observation room, Captain. She has preliminary results to share."

Lucian followed him down corridors that grew progressively colder, through security checkpoints that had been taken over by Choir personnel, into a part of the facility he had never visited. The observation room was small, clinical, dominated by a window that looked into a space beyond.

Speaks-Low was in that space.

Lucian had seen prisoners before. He had overseen interrogations, watched men and women break under pressure, witnessed the various ways the human spirit could be bent until it shattered. He thought he understood what he would see.

He was wrong.

The man in the room beyond the window was barely recognizable as human. He sat in a metal chair, restrained at wrists and ankles, his body slack in a way that suggested every muscle had surrendered. His eyes were open but unfocused, staring at nothing, seeing nothing. His lips moved constantly, forming words without sound, a stream of consciousness that had no beginning and no end.

Around his head, a metal framework held a series of devices that pulsed with soft light. The tuning apparatus. It was still active, still working, even though the subject had clearly stopped resisting hours ago.

"Remarkable, is he not?" Volk stood beside Lucian, her voice carrying the enthusiasm of a scientist discussing an interesting specimen. "The MNA trains their operatives well. He held longer than most. But the tuning always works in the end. The mind cannot maintain coherence against sustained harmonic disruption. It simply... disperses."

"What have you learned?" Lucian's voice sounded distant to his own ears, as if someone else were speaking.

"A great deal. The Bioweb's architecture. The resonance frequencies they use for long-distance communication. The locations of several key infrastructure nodes." Volk smiled. "And something else. Something unexpected. The MNA has internal divisions we did not know about. A faction that is developing weapons of its own, outside the knowledge of their governing council. They call themselves the Untethered."

Lucian felt the information land, felt its implications ripple outward. The Untethered. He had heard rumors, nothing concrete. Now the Choir had confirmation, had details, had everything Speaks-Low knew about a faction that might have been the MNA's best hope for matching Pale City aggression.

"That will be useful," he said, because something was expected.

"It will be more than useful. It will be decisive." Volk turned to face him fully. "The Nullwave deployment is proceeding. Within three weeks, we will strike at the eastern Bioweb network. But now we know to watch for the Untethered as well. If they attempt to retaliate, we will be ready."

Three weeks. Lucian filed the timeline away, another piece of information for the dead drop, assuming he survived long enough to use it.

"What happens to the subject now?" he asked.

"He has given us everything he knows. The tuning will continue for another day, perhaps two, to ensure nothing has been overlooked." Volk's tone was clinical, detached. "After that, he will be... non-functional. The mind does not recover from this level of disruption. We will transfer him to a long-term care facility, where he will live out his remaining years in a state of comfortable vacancy."

Comfortable vacancy. The words were obscene in their blandness. Speaks-Low would spend the rest of his life as an empty shell, his identity erased, his self dissolved, kept breathing by machines that could not restore what had been taken.

"The Renewal thanks you for your service, Captain." Volk turned back to the window, dismissing him. "You may return to your duties."

Lucian walked out of the observation room, through the corridors, back to his office. He sat at his desk and stared at the wall and felt something inside him finish dying.

He had tried to warn them. He had done everything he could. And it had not been enough.

The message in the dead drop would tell the MNA what had happened. They would know that Speaks-Low was lost, that the Choir had extracted everything, that the Nullwave was three weeks away. They would have to act on that information somehow.

But for Speaks-Low himself, there was nothing more to be done. The man who had been was already gone. What remained was a body that breathed and a mind that had been scattered like ash in wind.

Lucian sat in his office and listened to the silence from below, and wondered how many more people would have to be destroyed before this war finally ended.

Or if ending was even possible anymore.

The Cold War had just grown colder. And somewhere in the distance, the first tremors of something worse were beginning to build.

14

What Fathers Owe

The meeting place was a ruin on the frontier, three hours from the nearest Pale City outpost.

Rowan Halding arrived alone, against the advice of his security detail, against the protocols that governed every moment of a Prime Councillor's life. He had told them he needed time to think, that he would be walking the grounds of the old retreat where his family had spent summers when he was young. They had believed him because they wanted to believe, because questioning the Prime Councillor too closely was not conducive to career advancement.

The truth was simpler and more dangerous. His daughter had asked to see him. And despite everything, despite seven years of silence and public shame and private grief, he could not refuse.

The ruin had been a church once, in the days before the Doctrine Keepers had consolidated religious practice under state guidance. Its walls still stood, though the roof had long since collapsed, leaving the interior open to a sky that was beginning to color with sunset. Wildflowers grew between the broken pews. Birds nested in the empty window frames. Nature was reclaiming what humans had abandoned.

Marin was waiting for him inside.

She stood near what had been the altar, her back to the entrance, her posture the same proud stillness he remembered from her childhood. She had been seventeen when she left, barely more than a girl, full of questions he had not known how to answer and convictions he had tried to discourage. Now she was twenty-four, and the girl had become a woman he did not recognize.

She turned as he approached, and he saw his wife's eyes looking back at him from a face that had grown sharper, more defined. Elena had been dead for twelve years, taken by a sickness that the Pale Cities' medicine could not cure. Marin had her mother's eyes, her mother's stubborn jaw, her mother's way of standing as if she expected the world to bend around her.

"Father." Her voice was cool, controlled. "Thank you for coming."

"You asked." He stopped several meters away, maintaining distance. Trust was a bridge that had been burned long ago. "You said it was urgent."

"It is." She did not move closer either. "The Quiet Choir is preparing to deploy the Nullwave. You know this."

"I know."

"And you authorized their interrogation of the MNA commander. You gave them access to a man they will destroy."

"I had no choice." The words came out harder than he intended. "The Assembly was unanimous. The Choir's supporters have been gaining strength for months. If I had refused, I would have been removed, and whoever replaced me would have given them everything they wanted without hesitation."

"So you gave them what they wanted with hesitation. That makes it better?"

"It makes it survivable." Rowan felt the familiar exhaustion settling over him, the weight of compromises that had accumulated over years until they formed a burden he could barely carry. "You do not understand what it is like, Marin. You left. You chose to walk away from the responsibilities, the pressures, the impossible choices. I stayed. I have to live with the consequences of staying."

"I understand more than you think." She moved then, stepping down from the altar platform, walking toward him with measured steps. "I have spent seven years learning what the MNA actually is. Not the propaganda version, not the threat the Doctrine Keepers invented to keep people afraid. The real thing. A society that has found a way to live without destroying everything it touches."

"A society that would see us extinct."

"No." Her voice sharpened. "That is the lie, Father. That is the foundation of everything the Doctrine Keepers have built. The MNA does not want us extinct. They never did. They offered integration. They offered to share their knowledge, their land, their way of living. Our ancestors refused because integration meant equality, and they wanted dominance."

"That is MNA propaganda."

"That is history." Marin stopped an arm's length away, close enough that he could see the fine lines around her eyes, the weathering that came from living outdoors in a climate the Pale Cities' domes could not provide. "I have read the original documents. The actual records from the time of the Divergence, not the versions Drax's people have edited. I know what was offered and what was refused. I know why we live the way we do, and it is not because the MNA forced us into it."

Rowan wanted to argue. Wanted to defend the narrative he had believed all his life, the story that made sense of his world and his place in it. But looking at his daughter, at the certainty in her face, he found that the words would not come.

Because part of him had always suspected. Part of him had looked at the gaps in the official history, the questions that were never quite answered, the inconsistencies that the Doctrine Keepers glossed over with patriotic fervor. Part of him had known, and he had chosen not to know, because knowing would have made his life impossible.

"Why did you ask me here?" he said quietly.

"Because the Nullwave will kill thousands of people. Because the war the Choir is starting will kill thousands more. Because you are the only person in the Pale Cities who might be able to stop it." Marin's eyes held his, unflinching. "I am asking you to help us prevent a catastrophe."

"Help you how?"

"Delay the deployment. Find reasons, create obstacles, do whatever you have to do to buy time. The MNA is working on countermeasures, but they need weeks, not days." She reached into her jacket and produced a small device, holding it out to him. "And give us information. Deployment schedules. Target locations. Anything that can help us prepare."

Rowan stared at the device in her hand. It was a communicator, he realized. A way to contact her, or whoever she worked with now. A direct line to the enemy.

"You are asking me to commit treason."

"I am asking you to save lives." Her voice softened slightly. "I am asking you to be the man Mother believed you were. The man who used to tell me that leadership meant protecting people, not sacrificing them."

The mention of Elena hit him like a blow. He turned away, walking to one of the empty window frames, looking out at the frontier that stretched toward the horizon. Land that belonged to no one, that both sides claimed and neither truly controlled.

"If I do what you are asking, and I am discovered, I will be executed. The Halding name will be erased from history. Everything I have worked for will be destroyed."

"And if you do not do what I am asking, thousands will die. Maybe tens of thousands, if the war escalates the way the Choir wants it to." Marin's footsteps approached behind him. "The Halding name or innocent lives. That is the choice, Father. I cannot make it for you."

Rowan closed his eyes. He thought about the Assembly chamber, the faces of men and women who had trusted him to lead them. He thought about the Choir's laboratories, the sounds that came from interrogation rooms, the price that was being paid for the information they craved. He thought about Elena, who had died believing in him, and Marin, who had left because she could not.

He thought about what it meant to be a leader. What it had always meant, beneath the rhetoric and the ceremony and the carefully constructed image.

Protecting people. Not sacrificing them.

He turned and took the communicator from Marin's hand.

* * *

They talked until the stars emerged.

Not about politics or war or the desperate gamble they were undertaking. About other things. Smaller things. The years between them, the memories they shared, the people they had each become in the other's absence.

Marin told him about her life in the MNA. The work she did, helping people from the Pale Cities who wanted to integrate. The community she had found, the friendships she had built, the sense of belonging she had never felt at home. She spoke of forests that sang with the Bioweb's harmonics, of cities grown from living wood, of a relationship with the land that the Pale Cities had never imagined possible.

Rowan listened, and for the first time in years, he did not argue. He simply listened, letting her words paint a picture of a world he had been taught to fear but had never truly understood.

"Do you regret leaving?" he asked finally.

"I regret how I left. The things I said. The pain I caused you." She was quiet for a moment. "But leaving itself? No. I could not have become who I am if I had stayed. The Pale Cities would have crushed that out of me, the way they crush it out of everyone who asks too many questions."

"I asked questions once." The admission surprised him. "When I was young. Before I learned that questions were dangerous."

"What happened?"

"I was told that leadership required certainty. That doubt was weakness. That my role was to project confidence, not to seek truth." He looked at his daughter, at the woman she had become despite everything he had tried to make her. "I believed them. I spent forty years believing them. And now I am not sure what I believe anymore."

"That is a beginning." Marin's hand touched his arm, the first physical contact between them in seven years. "Uncertainty is not weakness, Father. It is honesty. The willingness to admit you do not know everything is the first step toward learning."

"I am too old to start learning."

"You are too old to keep pretending." Her grip tightened briefly, then released. "The man who gave me the communicator is not the same man who let me walk away seven years ago. Something has changed. Maybe it has been changing for a long time, and you just did not want to see it."

Rowan thought about the past months. The compromises that had grown harder to stomach. The Choir's demands that had grown harder to justify. The look in Julienne Drax's eyes when she spoke of necessary sacrifices, and the growing suspicion that the sacrifices would never stop, that they would only grow larger until everything had been fed to the machine she was building.

"Something has changed," he agreed. "I do not know if it is enough."

"It will have to be." Marin stepped back, the moment of connection ending as the reality of their situation reasserted itself. "I have to go. Staying longer is too dangerous for both of us."

"Will I see you again?"

"I do not know." She smiled, and for a moment she looked like the girl who had challenged him at dinner tables, who had refused to accept easy answers, who had loved him despite his failures. "But I hope so. When this is over. When we have built something worth seeing."

She walked away into the darkness, her footsteps fading until the night swallowed them completely. Rowan stood alone in the ruined church, holding a communicator that could end his life, and felt something he had not felt in years.

Hope. Fragile and uncertain, but real.

He tucked the device into his coat and began the long walk back to his vehicle, back to the capital, back to the life he would now have to live as a lie.

The stars wheeled overhead, indifferent to the small dramas of humans below. Somewhere to the west, the MNA was preparing for a war they hoped to prevent. Somewhere to the east, the Choir was preparing for a war they hoped to win.

And in between, on a frontier that belonged to no one, a father had chosen his daughter over his country.

He did not know if it was the right choice. He only knew it was the only choice he could live with.

That would have to be enough.

15

The Weight of Names

The message arrived at Wakana Station three hours before dawn.

Chogan was not sleeping. He had stopped sleeping through the night years ago, his body accustomed to the rhythms of crisis, his mind too restless to surrender to unconsciousness for more than a few hours at a time. He was reviewing the reports from the Elias extraction, noting the confirmation that intelligence had been compromised, when the secure channel activated with the particular frequency that meant urgent information from inside Pale City territory.

He read the message once. Then again. Then a third time, as if repetition might change the words.

It did not.

Choir has completed interrogation. Subject non-functional. All operational knowledge compromised. Nullwave deployment confirmed: three weeks. Target: eastern Bioweb network. Choir aware of Untethered. Recommend immediate countermeasures.

Subject non-functional. The clinical language could not disguise what it meant. Speaks-Low was gone. Not dead, which might have been kinder, but destroyed. His mind scattered by the Choir's devices, his self erased, his body left to breathe without purpose in some facility where the Pale Cities warehoused the people they had broken.

Chogan set the message down and stared at the wall of his quarters. The wall was grown from living wood, part of the grandmother oak that sheltered Wakana Station, its surface warm with the pulse of the Bioweb's harmonics. He had looked at this wall every morning for fifteen years. He had never noticed how beautiful it was until now, when he was trying not to think about a man who would never see anything beautiful again.

Speaks-Low. He had known him for thirty years. They had trained together as young Guardians, had served together on the frontier, had risen through the ranks in parallel paths that sometimes crossed and sometimes diverged. Speaks-Low had been the one to speak at Chogan's elevation to the diplomatic corps, had stood beside him when his wife passed, had sent quiet messages of support during the long years of negotiation and compromise that had worn Chogan down to what he was now.

And now he was gone. Not heroically, not in battle, not even in the clean finality of death. Simply erased, like a word rubbed from a page, leaving only a smudge where meaning had been.

The message had more. The Nullwave timeline. The target. The Choir's knowledge of the Untethered. All of it urgent, all of it demanding action, all of it secondary to the grief that Chogan could not afford to feel.

He stood, dressed in the formal robes that his position required, and prepared to tell the Rooted Council that one of their finest commanders had been destroyed and that war was three weeks away.

* * *

The Council chamber was a circle of living wood, grown over centuries into a space where the MNA's most important decisions were made.

Twelve seats arranged around a central hearth that burned with flames fed by the Bioweb's energy. Above, a dome of interwoven branches filtered the morning light into patterns that shifted with the wind. The chamber was designed to remind those who sat in it that they were part of something larger than themselves, that their decisions would echo through generations, that the land itself was listening.

Today, nine of the twelve seats were filled. Three representatives had not yet arrived from distant nations, delayed by the same weather that made the branches above sway and whisper. But the core members were present: the elders who guided policy, the war chiefs who commanded the Guardians, the keepers who maintained the Bioweb, the speakers who carried the voice of their peoples.

And in the center, standing where petitioners traditionally stood, Chogan Grayfeather prepared to deliver news that would change everything.

"The Quiet Choir has completed their interrogation of Commander Speaks-Low," he said. No preamble. No softening. The Council deserved the truth without decoration. "He has been rendered non-functional. His knowledge is now in enemy hands."

Silence. The kind of silence that falls when words are too heavy to be immediately processed. Chogan watched the faces around the circle: shock, grief, anger, fear. The full spectrum of responses to catastrophe.

Elder Makya, the oldest member of the Council, spoke first. Her voice was thin with age but carried the weight of authority. "What does 'non-functional' mean, precisely?"

"It means the Choir's interrogation techniques have destroyed his mind. He is alive but no longer present. He will never recover." Chogan forced himself to continue. "It also means that everything he knew is now available to our enemies. Bioweb architecture. Communication frequencies. Infrastructure locations. And the existence of the Untethered."

The reaction to that last word was immediate. Several Council members exchanged glances. War Chief Tahoma leaned forward, his scarred face hardening.

"The Untethered are known to the Choir?"

"They know they exist. They know they are developing weapons outside Council oversight. They will be watching for any attempt at retaliation." Chogan paused. "Our intelligence also indicates the Nullwave will be deployed within three weeks. The target is the eastern Bioweb network."

"Three weeks." Elder Makya's voice was barely a whisper. "That is not enough time."

"No. It is not." Chogan had spent the walk to the chamber calculating options, and none of them were good. "If the Nullwave strikes the eastern network, we lose communication with seven major settlements. Medical facilities will fail. Food distribution will collapse. The environmental systems that keep those regions habitable will begin to degrade."

"How many dead?" War Chief Tahoma asked.

"Immediately? Perhaps hundreds. In the following months, as systems fail and cannot be repaired? Thousands. Perhaps tens of thousands." Chogan met the War Chief's eyes. "This is not an act of war in the traditional sense. It is an attempt to cripple us without firing a shot. To make our way of life unsustainable."

"Then we strike first." The voice came from Councilor Waya, the youngest member of the body, a woman whose nation bordered Pale City territory and had suffered most in the decades of tension. "We use the Untethered's weapons. We show them that aggression has consequences."

"And then?" Elder Makya turned to face her. "We strike, they strike back, we strike again. Where does it end, Councilor? When both sides have destroyed each other? When the land we are sworn to protect has been poisoned by the weapons we built to defend it?"

"It ends when they understand they cannot defeat us. When the cost of aggression becomes too high to bear." Waya's voice was hard with conviction. "Diplomacy has failed. Negotiation has failed. Commander Speaks-Low is gone because we sent him to rescue prisoners from a facility that should never have existed. How many more must we lose before we admit that peace with these people is impossible?"

The chamber erupted into argument. Voices overlapped, positions clashed, the careful consensus that usually guided Council deliberations fracturing under the pressure of crisis. Chogan stood in the center and let it happen, knowing that the debate had to run its course before anything could be decided.

But as he listened, he noticed something. The arguments were familiar. The positions had been staked out years ago, hardening over time into factions that talked past each other rather than to each other. The hawks wanted retaliation. The doves wanted negotiation. And neither side could see that the world had changed, that the old categories no longer applied, that the choice before them was not war or peace but survival or extinction.

"There is another option," he said.

The chamber quieted. All eyes turned to him.

"We have assets inside the Pale Cities. People who have been providing intelligence, people who share our desire to prevent war." Chogan chose his next words carefully. "One of those assets has made contact with Prime Councillor Halding himself. There is reason to believe that factions within their government are working against the Choir, trying to delay or prevent the Nullwave deployment."

"You are suggesting we trust our survival to people who have already proven they cannot be trusted?" War Chief Tahoma's voice was skeptical.

"I am suggesting we pursue multiple paths simultaneously." Chogan turned to face the War Chief directly. "Yes, we prepare defenses. Yes, we develop countermeasures. Yes, we consider the Untethered's weapons as a last resort. But we also give our assets time to work. We give the factions inside the Pale Cities a chance to stop this before it starts."

"And if they fail?"

"Then we will have lost nothing but time. And time is what we need most." Chogan looked around the circle, meeting each pair of eyes in turn. "Three weeks is not enough to prepare defenses. It is not enough to evacuate settlements. It is not enough to build the countermeasures we need. But it might be enough for our assets to create obstacles, to delay deployment, to buy us the weeks we need to become ready."

Silence again. But a different kind this time. The silence of people considering rather than reacting.

Elder Makya spoke. "What do you propose, specifically?"

"I propose we send a message to our assets requesting

maximum interference with the Nullwave program. I propose we activate emergency protocols for the eastern network, beginning quiet evacuations and system redundancies that can minimize damage if the attack comes. I propose we open a back channel to the Untethered, not to authorize their weapons, but to coordinate our response." Chogan paused. "And I propose we continue the summit. Continue talking. Give the appearance of normalcy while we prepare for catastrophe."

"You are asking us to pretend nothing has changed while everything has changed," Councilor Waya said.

"I am asking us to be strategic. To use every tool available, including deception, to protect our people." Chogan felt the exhaustion of the past weeks settling into his bones, but he kept his voice steady. "We can mourn Speaks-Low when this is over. We can debate the failures that led us here when we have survived. But right now, we need to act, and we need to act in ways that give us the best chance of seeing tomorrow."

The Council deliberated. Voices rose and fell. Arguments were made and countered. But in the end, as the morning light shifted through the dome above, they reached consensus.

Chogan's proposals were approved. All of them.

* * *

He found Aiyana waiting for him outside the chamber.

She had returned from the extraction two days ago, her mission successful, her asset safely delivered to the debriefing teams. But something had changed in her since the detention facility, since the night she had left Speaks-Low behind. A hardness in her eyes that had not been there before. A weight in her posture that spoke of burdens she was not sharing.

"You heard," Chogan said. Not a question.

"I heard." Her voice was flat, controlled. "He is gone."

"He is gone." Chogan began walking, and she fell into step beside him. The corridors of the grandmother oak stretched around them, warm with morning light, alive with the sounds of a station preparing for another day. "The Council has authorized emergency measures. We have three weeks to prepare for something we may not be able to stop."

"What do you need from me?"

He considered the question. Considered what he had learned about her in recent weeks: the extraction she had led, the choices she had made, the reports from her team that spoke of a young woman becoming something harder and more capable than anyone had expected.

"The Untethered," he said. "You found them."

She stopped walking. Her expression did not change, but something shifted behind her eyes. "How did you know?"

"Because I know you. Because I know you would not have come back from that extraction unchanged unless you had learned something that forced you to see the world differently." He turned to face her. "And because the Council has asked me to contact them, and I do not know how."

Aiyana was silent for a long moment. When she spoke, her voice was careful, measured. "They showed me things. Weapons they have developed. Countermeasures to the Null-wave. A philosophy that says the Council's restraint is weakness, that the only language the Pale Cities understand is force."

"And what do you believe?"

"I believe the Council's restraint has cost us Speaks-Low." The words came out hard, edged with the grief she was not allowing herself to fully feel. "I believe negotiation has limits. I believe there are enemies who cannot be reasoned with, only stopped." She paused. "But I also believe the Untethered's path leads to becoming what we fight against. That weapons built for defense become weapons used for attack, and that once we cross that line, we cannot uncross it."

"A careful answer."

"An honest one." She met his eyes. "You want me to be your contact with them. To serve as a bridge between the Council and a faction that has rejected Council authority."

"Yes."

"Why me?"

"Because they trust you. Because you have seen what they are and did not immediately condemn them. Because you are young enough to understand why they exist and old enough to see why they are dangerous." Chogan felt the weight of his years pressing down on him. "And because I am too old for this fight, Aiyana. I can guide policy. I can advocate for paths I believe in. But the actual work of preventing catastrophe requires someone who can move between worlds, who can hold contradictions in her mind without breaking, who can do what needs to be done even when the right path is not clear."

"You are asking me to be a spy. An intermediary. A person who belongs to no faction because she serves all of them."

"I am asking you to be what our people need." His voice softened. "I know it is not fair. I know it is not the life you imagined for yourself. But the life any of us imagined ended when the Choir began building weapons that could destroy everything we have built. What remains is the life we must live to survive."

Aiyana looked away, toward a window where morning light streamed through leaves that were just beginning to turn with the season. Her eagle, Sitala, was somewhere out there, hunting in the forests that surrounded the station, feeling the freedom that her bonded partner could no longer afford.

"I will do it," she said. "I will contact the Untethered. I will serve as your bridge." She turned back to face him. "But I want something in return."

"Name it."

"The traitor. Someone inside the Alliance has been feeding information to the Pale Cities. The extraction codes that were compromised, the operational details that reached the enemy, the knowledge that let them set their trap. I want authorization to find them." Her eyes were hard. "I want to know who betrayed Speaks-Low."

Chogan considered the request. It was dangerous. Hunting for a traitor within their own ranks could destabilize the trust that held the Alliance together, could create suspicion where there should be cooperation, could damage the very unity they needed to survive the coming weeks.

But she was right. The traitor was real. And as long as they remained hidden, nothing the Alliance did was truly secure.

"You have it," he said. "Find them. But be careful. The traitor has access to our most sensitive operations. They will know if you are hunting them."

"Let them know." Aiyana's voice carried something cold, something that had not been there before Speaks-Low was taken. "Let them understand that someone is coming for them. Maybe they will make a mistake."

She turned and walked away, her footsteps silent on the woven floors. Chogan watched her go, watched the woman she was becoming disappear around a corner, and felt the particular grief of a mentor who has asked too much of someone too young.

But there was no one else. That was the truth of their situation. The experienced operatives were stretched thin. The Council was paralyzed by debate. The enemy was moving, and the only people with the freedom to act were those who had not yet learned that action always carries costs.

Aiyana would learn. That was the tragedy. She would learn, and the learning would change her, and whatever emerged on the other side would be something neither of them could predict.

Chogan turned toward his quarters, toward the messages waiting to be sent and the plans waiting to be made.

Three weeks. That was what they had. Three weeks to prevent a catastrophe, to find a traitor, to coordinate with factions that did not trust each other, to somehow hold together a world that was threatening to fly apart.

It was not enough time.

It would have to be.

16

The First Broadcast

The recording studio was grown from a single seed.

Elias stood in the center of it, surrounded by walls that curved like the inside of a shell, their surfaces alive with the soft pulse of Bioweb harmonics. The MNA technicians had explained the process: his words would be captured, encoded into frequencies that could ride the very infrastructure the Pale Cities used for their Signal Mesh, slipping past the censors through channels they did not know existed. His voice would reach receivers hidden in apartments and workshops across Nova-Providence, carried by the same technology that usually broadcast propaganda.

Poetic justice, they called it. Using the enemy's tools against them.

Elias called it terrifying.

"You do not have to do this." The woman beside him was named Saya, a communications specialist who had spent years building the network that would carry his message. She was older than him by a decade, her face lined with the particular exhaustion of someone who had been fighting this fight long before he joined it. "We can use other voices. Other defectors who have been here longer, who know how to speak to audiences who have been raised on lies."

"No." Elias shook his head. "It has to be me. I was inside the Cultural Ministry. I had access to the archives. When I speak about what I found, people will know I am not inventing it. They will recognize the details."

"Some will. Others will think you have been brainwashed. That the MNA has put words in your mouth." Saya's voice was gentle but honest. "You should know what you are walking into. The Doctrine Keepers have spent years inoculating people against exactly this kind of message. They have told your people that defectors are weak, corrupted, tools of the enemy. Your voice will confirm everything they have been taught to believe."

"For some. Not for all." Elias thought about Mira, about the underground network that had saved him, about all the people who were still hiding in the tunnels and safe houses of Nova-Providence, waiting for something to believe in. "There are people who are ready to hear the truth. They just need someone to say it out loud."

Saya studied him for a long moment. Then she nodded. "All right. We will begin whenever you are ready."

Elias took a breath. Then another. He thought about everything that had led him here: the books he had read, the questions he had asked, the long walk through tunnels where generations of truth-tellers had lived and died. He thought about Mira's parting words. *Make the truth matter.*

"I am ready," he said.

Saya activated the recording system. The walls hummed with a new frequency, capturing everything, preparing to send his words across a border that was supposed to be impenetrable.

Elias began to speak.

* * *

"My name is Elias Harren. Until three weeks ago, I worked in the Cultural Ministry of Nova-Providence, in the Department of Historical Preservation. My job was to catalog and maintain the archives that tell us who we are and where we come from."

He paused, letting the words settle. Somewhere across the border, receivers were activating. People were listening, some by choice, some by accident, some because they had been waiting years for a voice like his.

"I am speaking to you from MNA territory. The Doctrine Keepers will tell you I have been captured, tortured, forced to say these things. They will tell you I am a traitor, a weakling, a tool of the enemy. They will say anything to prevent you from hearing what I have to say."

"I am asking you to listen anyway. Not because I expect you to believe me. But because what I have learned deserves to be heard, and you deserve the chance to decide for yourself what is true."

Another pause. The walls pulsed around him, patient, waiting.

"We are taught that the Long March was a persecution. That our ancestors were driven from fertile lands by the savage alliance, forced to build new lives in hostile territory, victims of a cruelty that continues to this day. We are taught that the MNA wants us dead, that they have always wanted us dead, that the only thing standing between us and extinction is the strength of our walls and the unity of our purpose."

"I believed this. I believed it completely, the way you believe the ground beneath your feet is solid. It was the foundation of everything I understood about the world."

"And then I found the archives."

He told them about the documents. The original records from the time of the Divergence, preserved in restricted sections that most historians never accessed. The treaties that had been offered, the terms that had been proposed, the systematic rejection of every opportunity for peaceful coexistence.

"The MNA did not drive our ancestors away. They invited them to stay. They offered to share the land, the knowledge, the way of living that allowed them to thrive without destroying what sustained them. All they asked in return was that our ancestors accept certain limits. That they take only what could be renewed. That they participate in systems of balance rather than extraction."

"Our ancestors refused. Not because the terms were unfair. Not because they were being persecuted. But because they wanted more than balance allowed. They wanted dominance. They wanted the right to take without asking, to consume without consequence, to build empires that would stand above the land rather than within it."

"The Long March was not a persecution. It was a choice. Our ancestors chose to leave rather than accept equality. They chose to build the Pale Cities rather than live as partners with the people who were already here."

"Everything we have been taught since then has been designed to hide that choice. To make us believe we are victims when we are actually descendants of people who rejected an offer of peace because peace required them to share."

He could feel the weight of the words as they left him. Could feel them traveling outward, carried on frequencies that would slip past censors and reach ears that had been trained to reject exactly this message.

"I know this is difficult to hear. I know it contradicts everything you have been taught. I am not asking you to believe me blindly. I am asking you to look. To ask questions. To seek out the gaps in the stories you have been told, the inconsistencies that do not quite fit, the moments when the official narrative requires you to accept things that do not make sense."

"The truth is there, waiting to be found. The Doctrine Keepers have worked hard to bury it, but they cannot bury everything. If you look carefully enough, you will see what I saw. You will understand what I understand."

"And then you will have to make a choice. The same choice our ancestors made, in a different form. Do you want to live in a world built on lies? Or are you willing to face the truth, no matter how painful, and build something better?"

"I chose truth. I lost everything I had because of that choice. My home. My family. My entire life. But I do not regret it. Because a life built on lies is not really a life at all. It is just a comfortable prison that we agree not to notice."

"My name is Elias Harren. I am not your enemy. I am your neighbor, your cousin, someone who grew up in the same streets you walk, breathing the same filtered air, believing the same stories. The only difference between us is that I looked behind the curtain and saw what was there."

"Look for yourself. That is all I ask. Look, and decide what you see."

He stopped speaking. The walls continued to hum for a moment, then fell silent. The recording was complete.

* * *

Saya found him outside the studio, sitting on a bench beneath a tree whose leaves filtered the afternoon light into shifting patterns.

"The broadcast went out," she said, sitting beside him. "We are already receiving responses from our contacts inside the cities. People are listening."

"How many?"

"Impossible to know precisely. The Signal Mesh is designed to prevent accurate measurement of unauthorized transmissions." She paused. "But our estimates suggest several thousand receivers activated. In Nova-Providence alone."

Several thousand. Such a small number, set against the millions who lived in the Pale Cities. A drop in an ocean of propaganda, a whisper against a roar.

But drops became streams. Whispers became conversations. And conversations, given time, could become movements.

"The Doctrine Keepers will respond," Elias said. "They will denounce me. Call me a traitor, a puppet, everything you warned me about."

"They already are. Our monitors picked up an emergency broadcast thirty minutes after yours ended. Julienne Drax herself spoke." Saya's voice carried a note of grim satisfaction. "She was not pleased."

"What did she say?"

"The usual. That you were a disturbed individual who fell prey to enemy manipulation. That your claims are fabrications designed to weaken civic unity. That any citizen who listens to unauthorized transmissions is committing an act of disloyalty." Saya smiled slightly. "She mentioned you by name six times. She is afraid of you."

Afraid. Julienne Drax, the Chief Doctrine Keeper, the architect of decades of propaganda, afraid of one man's voice. Elias was not sure he believed it.

But he wanted to.

"What happens now?" he asked.

"Now we wait. We monitor reactions. We prepare the next broadcast." Saya turned to face him. "You told them to look for themselves. Some will. Most will not. But the ones who do, the ones who start asking questions, they will need more. More evidence. More context. More voices confirming what you said."

"I can provide that. I have more. So much more that I never got to say."

"Good. Because this is not a single battle. It is a long campaign. The Doctrine Keepers have had generations to build their narrative. We will not tear it down with one broadcast, or ten, or a hundred." Her eyes held his. "But every crack we make weakens the foundation. Every person who starts questioning makes space for others to question too. That is how change happens. Not in sudden revolutions, but in the slow accumulation of doubt."

Elias thought about the people he had left behind. His mother, who had taught him to be loyal. His father, who had taught him to be silent. His sister, who had stopped speaking to him because his questions made her uncomfortable.

Would any of them have heard his broadcast? Would any of them have listened? And if they listened, would they recognize the voice of someone they had once loved, or only hear the words of an enemy they had been trained to hate?

He did not know. He might never know.

But he had spoken. The words were out there now, traveling through channels he could not see, reaching ears he would never meet, planting seeds in minds that might or might not let them grow.

That was all he could do. Speak the truth and trust that somewhere, somehow, it would matter.

"Thank you," he said to Saya. "For giving me this chance."

"Thank yourself. You are the one who walked through tunnels for three days to get here. You are the one who gave up everything for the chance to speak." She stood, brushing leaves from her clothing. "Rest now. Tomorrow we begin planning the next message. And the one after that. And the one after that."

She walked away, leaving him alone beneath the tree. The light continued to shift overhead, the leaves dancing in a breeze that carried the scent of growing things. Somewhere in the distance, birds sang songs that had no meaning except beauty.

Elias sat and listened and let himself believe, for just a moment, that beauty might be enough.

That truth might be enough.

That the world he had left behind could still be saved.

17

Terms of Alliance

The Untethered compound looked different in daylight.

When Aiyana had first found this place, it had been shrouded in the strange frequencies of their experimental technology, its buildings half-hidden among ancient trees that seemed to lean away from the settlement as if uncertain of its presence. Now, landing in the clearing with Council authorization in her pocket and Sitala circling overhead, she could see it clearly: a community of perhaps fifty people, living in structures that blended MNA organic architecture with Pale City mechanical efficiency.

Gardens grew between workshops. Children played near sensor arrays that hummed with contained power. An elderly man sat on a porch, weaving something that looked like a net but resonated with frequencies Aiyana could feel through her sky-suit.

Not a military installation. A home.

Tavani was waiting for her at the edge of the clearing, arms crossed, expression unreadable. "You came back."

"I came back." Aiyana deactivated her sky-suit's flight

systems and walked toward the woman who had shown her weapons capable of devastating cities. "The situation has changed."

"I know. The Choir broke your commander. They know everything he knew, including that we exist." Tavani's voice was flat, factual. "Our scouts detected increased surveillance on all suspected Untethered locations within hours of his interrogation ending. The Council's policy of restraint has cost us our primary advantage: anonymity."

"The Council did not break Speaks-Low. The Choir did."

"The Council sent him into a situation where he could be captured. The Council failed to extract him before the Choir took over. The Council spent decades refusing to develop the countermeasures that might have prevented any of this." Tavani began walking toward the main settlement, not looking back to see if Aiyana followed. "Do not ask me to absolve them of responsibility. They had chances. They made choices. Those choices led here."

Aiyana followed, because following was the only way forward. The path wound between buildings where she glimpsed activity through windows: engineers working on devices, analysts studying screens, the constant quiet industry of people preparing for a conflict they believed was inevitable.

"The Council has authorized me to open negotiations," she said.

Tavani stopped walking. Turned. For the first time since Aiyana had arrived, something other than cold assessment showed in her eyes.

"Negotiations."

"Coordination, at minimum. They want to know what countermeasures you have developed against the Nullwave.

They want to discuss how our resources can be combined to protect the eastern network." Aiyana met her gaze steadily. "They are not offering legitimacy. They are not endorsing your methods. But they are acknowledging that we may need you."

"After fifteen years of pretending we do not exist." Tavani's laugh was short, bitter. "After denouncing us as dangerous radicals who threaten the balance. After sending security teams to harass our supply lines and infiltrate our operations. Now, when the war they refused to prepare for is three weeks away, they want to coordinate."

"Yes."

"And you? What do you want, Aiyana Waketah?" Tavani stepped closer, her intensity radiating like heat. "You came here once and walked away. You could have reported us then and chose not to. Now you return with the Council's blessing. But I do not believe you are simply a messenger. I do not believe you are content to carry words between factions and call it service."

Aiyana considered how much to reveal. Tavani was dangerous, unpredictable, driven by convictions that did not align neatly with Council policy. But she was also right about many things. And the mission Chogan had given her required honesty, or at least as much honesty as the situation could bear.

"I want to stop the Nullwave," she said. "I want to find the traitor who has been feeding information to the Pale Cities. I want to make sure that what happened to Speaks-Low never happens to anyone else." She paused. "And I am beginning to believe that the Council's way may not be enough to accomplish any of those things."

"Beginning to believe." Tavani's expression softened

slightly. "That is more honest than I expected."

"I am not ready to abandon everything the Council stands for. I still believe in balance. I still believe that what we are protecting matters more than how we protect it." Aiyana thought about the weapons she had seen in Tavani's workshop, the resonance amplifier that could bring the Pale Cities to their knees. "But I also believe that protection requires tools the Council has refused to develop. And I believe that if we do not work together, all of us, we are going to lose everything."

Tavani was quiet for a long moment. Around them, the compound continued its quiet activity, people moving with purpose, children laughing somewhere out of sight, the hum of technology that existed nowhere else in MNA territory.

"Come with me," she said finally. "There are things you need to see before we talk about terms."

* * *

The countermeasure laboratory was buried beneath the compound's main building.

Aiyana followed Tavani down a spiral staircase carved into living rock, the walls gradually transitioning from organic growth to something older, harder, more permanent. The Bioweb's harmonics faded as they descended, replaced by frequencies she did not recognize: the signature of technology that had evolved along a different path.

"We did not set out to build weapons," Tavani said as they walked. "When the Untethered first formed, we were researchers. Engineers who believed the Council was being too cautious, too conservative, too afraid of what our technology might become. We wanted to push boundaries. To explore possibilities that the official programs refused to consider."

"What changed?"

"The Wind Spine incident." Tavani's voice hardened. "When the Choir tested their prototype Nullwave and the Council's response was to negotiate. To send diplomats instead of demands. To treat an act of war as a misunderstanding that could be resolved through conversation." She pushed open a heavy door at the bottom of the stairs. "That was when we understood. The Council would never act until it was too late. If we wanted to survive, we would have to prepare ourselves."

The laboratory beyond the door was vast and humming with power. Workstations lined the walls, each focused on a different project. Aiyana saw defensive shields that could disperse Nullwave frequencies. Communication systems hardened against disruption. Medical equipment designed to treat injuries the Bioweb could not heal.

And in the center, surrounded by monitoring equipment and power conduits, the resonance amplifier she had seen on her first visit. But now she could see it more clearly: not just a weapon, but a system. A network of interconnected components that could channel the Bioweb's energy in ways the original designers had never intended.

"The amplifier can operate in two modes," Tavani said, leading her toward the central device. "Offensive: we project disruptive frequencies into Pale City territory, crippling their infrastructure. Defensive: we create a harmonic barrier that can absorb and redirect incoming Nullwave energy." She paused beside a control panel covered in displays Aiyana could not read. "We have never tested the defensive mode against a full-scale Nullwave attack. We do not know if it will work."

"But it might."

"It might." Tavani's eyes held hers. "The question is whether the Council will let us try. Whether they will accept help from people they have spent years condemning. Whether their pride is more important than our survival."

"The Council is afraid of what you represent," Aiyana said slowly. "Not just the weapons. The philosophy. The idea that restraint is weakness, that we should become more like our enemies to defeat them."

"And are they wrong to be afraid?" Tavani's question was genuine, not rhetorical. "I have asked myself that question every day for fifteen years. Every time we build something new, every time we push further into territory the Council has forbidden, I ask myself: are we becoming what we fight against? Are we losing ourselves in the name of saving ourselves?"

"What answer do you find?"

"I find that the question matters more than the answer." Tavani turned away from the amplifier, walking toward a section of the laboratory where screens displayed maps of MNA territory, the eastern network highlighted in red. "The Choir does not ask that question. Drax does not ask it. They have certainty, which means they have stopped thinking. We still doubt. We still question. That is what makes us different from them, even when we use similar tools."

Aiyana thought about the Council chamber, about the debates that had raged while Speaks-Low was being destroyed. About Councilor Waya's demand for retaliation and Elder Makya's insistence on restraint. About Chogan's exhausted compromise, trying to hold together factions that no longer spoke the same language.

The Council asked questions too. But their questions had become rituals, debates that circled without reaching conclusions, a performance of deliberation that had replaced actual decision-making.

Maybe that was what Tavani understood that the Council did not. Questions only mattered if they led to action. Doubt was only valuable if it sharpened choices rather than paralyzed them.

"What do you want from the Council?" she asked. "If they agree to coordinate. What do you actually need?"

"Access to the eastern network's infrastructure. We need to integrate our defensive systems with the existing Bioweb nodes if the barrier is going to work." Tavani pulled up a schematic on one of the screens. "Legitimacy for our engineers to operate openly. We have people who could be helping prepare evacuations, hardening systems, training response teams. They are hiding instead, because the Council has made our existence illegal."

"Is that all?"

"No." Tavani turned to face her fully. "I want a seat at the table. Not for myself. For the Untethered as a faction. A voice in the decisions that will shape how we respond to this attack and the ones that will follow. The Council has made choices about our future without us for too long. If we are going to risk our lives defending their policies, we deserve to help make them."

It was a significant demand. Bringing the Untethered into official governance would change the balance of power in the Council, would validate everything they had done, would shift the MNA's fundamental orientation toward preparedness and away from restraint.

But it was also, Aiyana realized, necessary. The world had changed. The old categories no longer applied. Either the MNA adapted or it died.

"I will carry your terms to the Council," she said. "I cannot promise they will accept."

"I know." Tavani's expression softened slightly. "But the fact that you came, that they sent you, that the door is open at all. That is more than we have had in fifteen years." She extended her hand. "Whatever happens, Aiyana Waketah, you have my respect. You are trying to hold together a world that wants to fly apart. That takes more courage than building weapons."

Aiyana took the hand. The grip was firm, calloused, the hand of someone who built things with her own fingers.

"There is one more thing," she said. "The traitor. The one feeding information to the Pale Cities. Do you have any idea who it might be?"

Tavani's expression shifted. Something dark moved behind her eyes.

"We have been investigating for months. We have narrowed the possibilities." She released Aiyana's hand. "But I am not ready to share what we have found. Not until I am certain. Accusing someone of treason without proof would destroy any chance of cooperation between our factions."

"You know something."

"I suspect something. There is a difference." Tavani began walking back toward the stairs. "Find me proof, and I will tell you everything. Until then, be careful whom you trust. The traitor has access to operations at the highest level. They could be anyone."

Aiyana followed her up the stairs, back into daylight, carrying questions that felt heavier than answers.

The Untethered had countermeasures that might save the eastern network. They had demands that might reshape MNA governance. They had suspicions about the traitor that they were not ready to share.

And somewhere, hidden among allies or enemies or both, someone was still feeding information to people who wanted to destroy everything.

Aiyana launched into the sky with Sitala beside her, carrying Tavani's terms back to a Council that would have to decide, very quickly, what kind of future they were willing to fight for.

The clock was running. Three weeks had become two.

Time enough for hope. Barely enough for action.

Not nearly enough for certainty.

18

The Keeper of Stories

The archive beneath the Doctrine Ministry stretched for kilometers.

Julienne Drax walked its corridors alone, as she did every evening when the weight of her work became too heavy to bear in the presence of others. The shelves rose around her like canyon walls, filled with documents that told the story of her people: the story she had spent forty years shaping, protecting, perfecting.

Most of these documents would never be read. They existed as raw material, the ore from which official history was refined. Contradictory accounts. Inconvenient details. The messy truth that had to be processed before it could be presented to citizens who needed clarity, not complexity.

Elias Harren had been here. Had walked these same corridors, touched these same shelves, read documents he should never have been able to access. And now he was broadcasting their contents to anyone with a hidden receiver, unraveling decades of careful work with every word he spoke.

Drax stopped before a section marked with symbols that

meant nothing to anyone who did not know the code. The restricted materials. The documents that contained the truth about the Divergence, the Long March, the choices that had shaped everything that followed.

She had read them all, years ago, when she first took this position. She had understood, then, why her predecessors had hidden them. Why the story had to be shaped. Why truth, in its raw form, was a poison that would destroy everything the Pale Cities had built.

People needed enemies. They needed to believe they were victims, that their struggles were inflicted from outside rather than consequences of choices made long ago. Take that belief away and what remained? A society built on a rejection of partnership, a refusal to share, a demand for dominance that had led to centuries of self-inflicted suffering.

The MNA had offered integration. That was the truth. They had offered to share their land, their knowledge, their way of living. And Drax's ancestors had refused because sharing meant limits. Because partnership meant equality. Because they had wanted to take without asking and build without permission and grow without constraint.

Now Elias Harren was telling that truth to anyone who would listen. And Drax had to find a way to make the truth not matter.

* * *

The emergency meeting convened in the Ministry's secure conference room, deep enough underground that no signal could penetrate.

Drax took her seat at the head of the table and surveyed the faces around her. Director Vance from Intelligence, looking smug about the success of the Choir's interrogation. General Thorn from the Border Guard, stone-faced as always. Minister

Callas from Civic Unity, nervous about the social implications of unauthorized broadcasts. And, at the far end of the table, Prime Councillor Halding himself, his expression carefully neutral.

She had known Rowan for thirty years. Had watched him rise through the ranks, had guided his education in the realities of governance, had believed he understood what was necessary to maintain the stability they had built. But lately, something had shifted. He asked questions he should not ask. He hesitated where he should act. He looked at her sometimes with an expression she could not read.

She would have to watch him. But that was a concern for later. Now, there was a more immediate problem to address.

"The Harren broadcast has reached approximately twelve thousand receivers in Nova-Providence alone," she began. "Our monitoring systems have detected similar reception patterns in New Albion and Ironbridge. The message is spreading through unauthorized networks faster than we can suppress it."

"Then suppress harder." General Thorn's voice was a growl. "Raid the networks. Arrest anyone caught with an unauthorized receiver. Make examples."

"We have been making examples for decades, General. The networks persist because people want them to persist. Every receiver we confiscate creates a martyr. Every arrest creates sympathy." Drax kept her voice measured, patient. Thorn was useful, but he understood only force. "Suppression is necessary but insufficient. We need a counter-narrative."

"What counter-narrative?" Minister Callas leaned forward, his anxiety evident. "Harren is telling people to look at the archives themselves. To find the gaps in our stories. If they look..."

"They will find what we want them to find." Drax smiled, the expression carrying no warmth. "The archives have been curated for generations. The documents Harren accessed were an oversight, a failure of compartmentalization that has since been corrected. Anyone who goes looking now will find evidence that confirms our narrative, not his."

"And the original documents? The ones he read?"

"Destroyed. As of this morning." Drax watched the reactions around the table. Relief from Callas. Approval from Thorn. Nothing from Vance, who understood that intelligence required flexibility. And from Halding, a flicker of something that might have been dismay, quickly suppressed. "Harren can claim to have read them, but he cannot prove they existed. It becomes his word against ours. And we have forty years of carefully constructed credibility on our side."

"What about his claims specifically?" Halding's voice was quiet, thoughtful. "The Long March narrative. The offer of integration. He is telling a specific story. How do we counter it?"

Drax studied him for a moment before answering. The question was reasonable, but the way he asked it. As if he were genuinely curious about the truth rather than focused on its management.

"We acknowledge a kernel of truth and wrap it in context," she said. "Yes, the MNA offered integration. But integration meant subjugation. Meant abandoning our identity, our values, our way of life. Our ancestors refused not because they were greedy, but because they were proud. Because they would not bow to a foreign power that demanded they become something other than what they were."

"Is that true?" Halding asked.

The question hung in the air. Around the table, the other officials shifted uncomfortably. This was not a question that was asked in these meetings. Truth was not the point. Effectiveness was the point.

"It is true enough," Drax said carefully. "The MNA's terms required significant changes to how our ancestors lived. Whether those changes constituted subjugation or simply adjustment is a matter of interpretation. We choose the interpretation that serves our people's sense of identity and purpose."

"And if our people choose a different interpretation?"

"Then we have failed in our duty to guide them." Drax's voice hardened. "Prime Councillor, I understand that the current crisis creates pressure to question our methods. But this is precisely the moment when we must hold firm. Harren's broadcast is dangerous because it offers an alternative story. If we waver, if we show uncertainty, we create space for that alternative to take root."

"I am not wavering." Halding's expression closed. "I am asking questions. Surely questions are not forbidden, even in this room."

"Questions are never forbidden. But they must be asked with purpose, not doubt." Drax held his gaze. "We are at war, Prime Councillor. The Nullwave deployment is two weeks away. The MNA is preparing countermeasures. And now we have a defector broadcasting propaganda into our cities. This is not the time for philosophical inquiry. This is the time for action."

The room was silent. Drax could feel the tension, the unspoken conflicts that ran beneath the surface of every meeting. Halding was not the man he had been. Something had changed him. Someone had reached him.

She would find out who. And she would deal with them.

"Director Vance," she said, turning away from Halding. "What do we know about the channels carrying Harren's broadcast?"

"They are using our own Signal Mesh infrastructure," Vance said. "Piggybacking on frequencies we did not know existed. The MNA has been building this network for years, right under our noses. We are working to identify and close the vulnerabilities, but it will take time."

"Time we may not have. What about the source? Can we trace where Harren is broadcasting from?"

"Not precisely. Somewhere in MNA territory, obviously. But the signal bounces through multiple relay points. By the time we trace one, they have shifted to another." Vance's tone carried professional admiration. "Whoever designed their communication system knew what they were doing."

"Then we focus on the receiving end. Identify clusters of unauthorized receivers. Map the underground networks. When the Nullwave deploys, we can use the chaos to clean house." Drax looked around the table. "The attack on the MNA will create disruption here as well. People will be afraid, uncertain. That is the moment to act against internal enemies. Fear focuses attention. It creates willingness to sacrifice liberty for security."

"You want to use the Nullwave as cover for a purge." Halding's voice was flat.

"I want to use every tool available to protect our society." Drax met his eyes without flinching. "The underground networks are a cancer. They have been growing for decades, spreading doubt, undermining unity. Harren's broadcast is a symptom, not a cause. If we do not excise the disease, it will consume us from within."

"And how many people will that excision cost?"

"As many as necessary. As few as possible." Drax stood, signaling that the meeting was ending. "I will prepare a detailed plan for the post-deployment security operations. General Thorn, I will need your support for enforcement. Director Vance, continue working on the communication vulnerabilities. Minister Callas, prepare messaging for the civilian population emphasizing unity and vigilance."

The officials rose, gathering their materials, moving toward the door. Halding remained seated.

"A word, Chief Keeper?" he said quietly.

Drax waited until the others had left, then closed the door and turned to face him.

"You are concerned about something, Prime Councillor."

"I am concerned about many things." Halding stood slowly, moving to the window that looked out on nothing but reinforced concrete. "The Nullwave. The purges you are planning. The direction we are heading."

"These concerns are new."

"Perhaps I have been suppressing them. Perhaps recent events have made suppression impossible." He turned to face her. "Julienne, we have known each other a long time. I have trusted your guidance, your judgment, your vision of what our society needs. But I am beginning to wonder if we have lost our way."

"Lost our way to what?"

"To something worth preserving." His voice was heavy with exhaustion. "The Nullwave will kill thousands. The purges will kill more. We will emerge from this crisis as a society that has sacrificed everything it claimed to value in the name of survival. Is that a victory?"

Drax considered her response carefully. She could dismiss his concerns, push back, remind him of his duty. That had worked before. But something in his tone suggested it would not work now. Something had fundamentally shifted.

"Survival is the prerequisite for everything else," she said. "We cannot build a better society if we do not exist. The MNA would destroy us if they could. The Nullwave is our response to that threat. The purges are our response to internal weakness. Neither is pleasant. Both are necessary."

"And if the threat is not what we have been told? If the MNA is not the enemy we have made them into?"

"Then we have been wrong for generations, and nothing we do now matters." Drax's voice sharpened. "Is that what you believe, Rowan? That everything we have built is based on a lie? That we should lay down our weapons and beg the savages for forgiveness?"

"I believe we should ask questions. I believe we should consider possibilities we have refused to consider." He moved toward the door. "I believe we should be very careful about the path we are choosing, because some paths cannot be walked back."

He left without waiting for her response. Drax stood alone in the conference room, surrounded by the silence of a bunker designed to survive catastrophe, and felt something she had not felt in decades.

Doubt.

Not doubt about her methods. Not doubt about the necessity of what they were doing. But doubt about the man she had trusted to lead them. Doubt about whether Rowan Halding was still the ally she needed him to be.

She activated her secure communicator and sent a message to her most trusted operative.

Watch the Prime Councillor. Report everything. Trust no one.

The game had changed. The pieces were moving in ways she had not anticipated. But Julienne Drax had not survived forty years in the shadows by being unprepared.

If Halding had become a liability, she would deal with him the way she dealt with all liabilities.

Quietly. Efficiently. Completely.

19

The Shape of Absence

The pattern emerged at three in the morning, when Aiyana's eyes were burning and her mind had reached the particular clarity that came from exhaustion.

She had been reviewing operational records for days, cross-referencing mission briefings with outcomes, tracking the flow of information from its origin to its destination. Renna's logic guided her: the traitor had access to both Elias's intelligence and the Council's operational planning. That narrowed the field. But narrowing was not the same as identifying.

The records were stored in Wakana Station's secure archive, a room grown from the grandmother oak's deepest roots, its walls resonating with frequencies designed to prevent unauthorized access. Aiyana had been given clearance by Chogan, clearance that let her see things most Guardians never saw: the full scope of operations conducted over the past year, the names of everyone involved, the chains of communication that connected field teams to command.

She had started by looking for what was present. Who knew about the detention facility extraction. Who had access to the codes Elias provided. Who attended the Council sessions where operational details were discussed.

The lists were long. Too long. Dozens of people had some level of access to each piece of information. Cross-referencing produced a smaller set, but still too large to be useful. The traitor could be any of fifteen people, all of them trusted, all of them with legitimate reasons to know what they knew.

So she changed her approach. Instead of looking for presence, she looked for absence.

What operations had not been compromised? What intelligence had reached its destination intact? What missions had succeeded despite the traitor's access to information that should have doomed them?

The pattern that emerged was subtle. Almost invisible. But once she saw it, she could not unsee it.

There were three operations in the past year that had proceeded without any sign of enemy foreknowledge. Three missions where the MNA had achieved complete surprise, where the Pale Cities had been caught entirely unprepared. In each case, the operational planning had followed the same unusual path: briefings conducted in person rather than through Bioweb channels, documentation kept to an absolute minimum, a specific subset of Council members excluded from the final planning sessions.

Excluded. Not because they lacked clearance. Because someone had decided, for reasons that were never documented, that they did not need to know.

Aiyana pulled the records for those three operations and compared the exclusion lists. Two names appeared on all three.

Elder Makya. And Councilor Waya.

She stared at the names, feeling the weight of what they

implied. Elder Makya, the oldest member of the Council, the voice of restraint and wisdom. Councilor Waya, the youngest, the voice of action and urgency. Two people who seemed to represent opposite poles of MNA politics, who argued against each other in every session, who appeared to have nothing in common except their positions of power.

One of them was the traitor. Or both. Or neither, and the pattern was coincidence, and she was seeing shapes in random noise because she was desperate for an answer.

She needed more. She needed to understand why those two had been excluded, who had made the decision, what reasoning had guided it.

She needed to talk to someone who had been there.

* * *

Chogan was awake, as she had known he would be.

She found him in his quarters, sitting by a window that looked out over the forest canopy, a cup of something warm cradled in his hands. The pre-dawn light was just beginning to touch the eastern sky, painting the clouds in shades of gray and rose.

"You have found something," he said without turning. His voice carried the particular fatigue of someone who had stopped expecting rest.

"I have found a pattern." Aiyana moved to stand beside him, looking out at the same view. "Three operations in the past year that were not compromised. In each case, two Council members were excluded from final planning. The same two members each time."

"Makya and Waya."

She turned to look at him. His expression had not changed, but something in the quality of his stillness told her this was not news to him.

"You knew."

"I suspected." He finally turned to face her, and she saw how much the past weeks had cost him. The lines around his eyes had deepened. His shoulders carried a weight that had nothing to do with physical burden. "The exclusions were my doing. Quiet arrangements, never documented, based on patterns I noticed but could not prove."

"Why did you not tell me?"

"Because suspicion is not evidence. Because accusing a Council member of treason without proof would destroy whatever unity we have left." He set down his cup and stood, moving to pace the small space of his quarters. "And because I was not certain which of them it was. The pattern suggested one of the two. It did not tell me which."

"Makya has been on the Council for forty years. She is the voice of restraint, of negotiation, of patience." Aiyana thought through the implications. "If she is the traitor, then her advocacy for peace has been a cover. Every argument she has made for diplomacy has been designed to buy time for our enemies."

"Or she genuinely believes in peace and is entirely innocent, and her exclusion from those operations was a mistake that cost her reputation with whoever made the decisions." Chogan's voice was heavy. "That is the problem with suspicion. It corrupts everything it touches. Once you suspect someone, every action they take can be interpreted as evidence of guilt."

"And Waya?"

"Waya argues for action. For retaliation. For meeting force with force." Chogan stopped pacing and faced her. "If she is the traitor, then her advocacy for war is designed to push us into a conflict we cannot win. To make us overreach, exhaust our resources, destroy ourselves in the name of fighting back."

"Or she genuinely believes we should fight and is entirely innocent."

"Or that." Chogan returned to his chair, sinking into it with visible exhaustion. "You see the problem. Both interpretations fit. Both are plausible. And without proof, accusing either of them would be catastrophic."

Aiyana thought about what Tavani had said. *Find me proof, and I will tell you everything.* The Untethered had been investigating too. They had narrowed the possibilities. Maybe they had found something she had not.

"The Untethered know something," she said. "Tavani told me they have been investigating for months. She would not share what they found, but she implied they have suspects."

"The Untethered have their own agenda. Their information may be accurate, or it may be designed to serve their interests." Chogan's voice carried warning. "Be careful about trusting them too completely. They want a seat at the Council table. Exposing a traitor among current Council members would serve that goal, whether the accusation is true or not."

"You think they might frame someone?"

"I think they might genuinely believe someone is guilty based on incomplete evidence, and their belief might be wrong." He met her eyes. "I also think they might be right. I do not know. That is the torture of this situation. Everyone has reasons. Everyone has motives. And the truth hides behind a wall of plausibility that I cannot penetrate."

Aiyana stood in the growing light and felt the weight of what she was being asked to do. Hunt for a traitor among people she had been taught to trust. Doubt everyone. Trust no one. Become, in some sense, the very thing she was hunting: someone who worked in shadows, who deceived those around her, who served a purpose that justified the means.

"There is another way," she said slowly. "A way to find proof without accusation."

"I am listening."

"We set a trap. We create false intelligence, something valuable enough that the traitor would want to pass it along. We give that intelligence to Makya alone, and different intelligence to Waya alone. Then we watch to see which version reaches the Pale Cities."

Chogan was quiet for a long moment. "That would work," he said finally. "If we had time. If we could afford to wait for the information to travel and be acted upon. But the Nullwave deploys in less than two weeks. By the time we confirmed which of them leaked, it might be too late."

"Then we accelerate the timeline. We make the intelligence urgent. Something that demands immediate action, that the traitor would have to pass along quickly or lose the opportunity."

"Such as?"

Aiyana thought. What would be valuable enough to force the traitor's hand? What would the Pale Cities pay any price to know?

"The Untethered's location," she said. "We tell Makya that we have discovered the Untethered compound and are planning a raid to confiscate their weapons. We tell Waya that we have made a deal with the Untethered and are integrating their countermeasures into our eastern network defenses." She paused. "Both pieces of information are valuable. Both would change Pale City planning. And they are different enough that we would know immediately which one leaked."

"You would be using the Untethered as bait."

"I would be using false information about the Untethered as bait. Their actual location, their actual capabilities, would remain secret." Aiyana met his eyes. "Tavani would have to agree. She would have to trust that we would not actually betray them. But if she wants a seat at the Council table, she has to demonstrate that she can work with us. This would be a test of that trust."

Chogan considered. She could see him weighing the risks, the possibilities, the ways this could go wrong. The ways it could go right.

"Do it," he said. "Talk to Tavani. If she agrees, we proceed. But be careful, Aiyana. If the traitor realizes they are being tested, they may act in ways we cannot predict. They may have contingencies we know nothing about."

"I understand."

"Do you?" His voice was gentle but serious. "You are playing a game against an opponent who has been playing longer than you have been alive. They have survived this long by being careful, by anticipating threats, by staying one step ahead. Do not assume you are smarter than they are. Do not assume you have thought of everything they have thought of."

"I will not."

"Good." He stood again, moving to look out the window at the sun now fully rising over the forest. "Go. Set your trap. Find our traitor. And pray to whatever you believe in that we are not too late."

Aiyana left him there, silhouetted against the morning light, carrying a burden she was only beginning to understand.

The hunt was narrowing. The shape of the enemy was

emerging from the shadows.

But shapes could be deceiving. And the closer she got to the truth, the more dangerous the truth became.

She flew toward the Untethered compound with Sitala beside her, carrying a plan that might save them all or might destroy everything.

There was only one way to find out.

20

Convergence

The Nullwave deployment facility was located in the industrial district of Nova-Providence, disguised as a power generation plant.

Lucian had learned its location three days ago, when a routine security rotation placed him in temporary command of the facility's perimeter detail. He had walked its corridors, noted its access points, memorized its guard schedules. He had done everything a loyal officer would do, and nothing that would raise suspicion.

Now he stood in the shadow of a maintenance building across the street, watching the facility's main entrance, waiting for the signal that would tell him it was time to act.

The message from the underground had been brief. *Asset in position. Distraction will occur at 0300. You will have twelve minutes.* Twelve minutes to enter the facility, reach the Nullwave control systems, and introduce the corruption that the MNA's technical specialists had designed. Twelve minutes to sabotage the weapon that would devastate the eastern Bioweb network and kill thousands.

Twelve minutes that would determine whether he lived as a hero or died as a traitor.

His chronometer showed 0258. Two minutes.

Lucian thought about his sister. About Lena, who had died because the frontier settlement where they grew up lacked resources that the core cities hoarded. He had joined the Border Guard to change that. To serve a system that he believed, once, could be reformed from within. To protect his people.

He still wanted to protect his people. He just understood, now, that the system he served was designed to make protection impossible. That the Pale Cities' leaders did not want reform. They wanted control. They wanted weapons like the Nullwave, tools of devastation that could be pointed at enemies but could never solve the problems that made enemies necessary.

0259.

He checked his equipment one final time. The data chip containing the corruption code, hidden in a pocket that scanners would not detect. The security credentials that his position gave him, legitimate access that would not raise alarms. The small disruptor that the underground had provided, capable of disabling electronic locks for exactly thirty seconds.

Everything was ready. Everything except his courage.

0300.

The explosion came from the eastern side of the facility, a controlled detonation that produced more light and noise than actual damage. The distraction. Guards began running toward the sound, shouting into communicators, following protocols that pulled them away from the entrances Lucian needed.

He moved.

* * *

The corridors of the facility were cold and sterile, lit by harsh artificial light that cast no shadows.

Lucian walked with the confidence of a man who belonged, his uniform opening doors that would have stopped anyone else. Guards he passed nodded in recognition. Technicians stepped aside to let him through. His presence here was unusual but not alarming; facility commanders occasionally made inspection rounds during security events.

The control room was on the third sublevel, behind a door that required both credentials and biometric confirmation. Lucian pressed his hand to the scanner, felt the brief tingle of the verification process, watched the door slide open.

Inside, banks of equipment hummed with contained power. Screens displayed status readouts that he had been taught to interpret during his security briefing. The Nullwave generator itself was in an adjacent chamber, a massive structure of coils and capacitors that could produce frequencies capable of disrupting any technology that relied on harmonic resonance.

The control console was unattended. The skeleton crew that normally monitored the systems had been drawn away by the explosion, leaving the room empty except for Lucian and the weapon that could end thousands of lives.

He had eight minutes left.

The data chip slid into the console's interface port with a soft click. Code began to flow, the corruption spreading through the Nullwave's targeting systems, introducing errors that would not be detectable until the weapon was actually fired. When deployment came, the frequencies would be wrong. The resonance patterns would fail to synchronize. The devastating pulse that was supposed to shatter the eastern Bioweb would instead dissipate harmlessly, a thunder that produced no lightning.

The progress indicator crept upward. Forty percent. Fifty. Sixty.

The door behind him opened.

Lucian spun, his hand moving toward his sidearm, and found himself facing Major Kellam. The same officer who had interrogated him about Renna's escape. The same cold eyes that had studied him with suspicion for months.

"Captain Ford." Kellam's voice was soft, almost gentle. "I had wondered when you would make your move."

"Major. I was conducting a security inspection. The explosion seemed like an appropriate time to verify our protocols."

"Of course you were." Kellam stepped into the room, letting the door close behind him. His hand rested on his weapon, but he did not draw. "And the data chip currently uploading to our targeting systems? That is part of the inspection as well?"

Lucian glanced at the console. Seventy-five percent. He needed more time.

"I do not know what you mean."

"Please, Captain. Let us not waste each other's time." Kellam began walking slowly around the room's perimeter, maintaining distance, keeping his eyes on Lucian. "I have suspected you since the Renna incident. No proof, of course. Just the instinct that something was not right. You were too competent, too careful, too precisely what a loyal officer should be. Real loyalty is messier. It makes mistakes."

Eighty percent.

"So you followed me."

"I followed you." Kellam stopped moving, positioning himself between Lucian and the door. "I watched you receive dead-drop communications. I saw you pass information to contacts I could not identify. I built a case, slowly, carefully, waiting for the moment when you would expose yourself completely."

"And now?"

"Now I have everything I need. You, alone in the Nullwave control room, uploading unauthorized code to our most important weapon. The evidence is irrefutable." Kellam's hand tightened on his weapon. "The question is what happens next."

Eighty-five percent.

"What do you want, Major?"

"I want to understand." For the first time, something other than cold suspicion showed in Kellam's eyes. Something that might have been genuine curiosity. "You had a career. A future. You could have risen to command the entire Border Guard, if you had stayed loyal. Why throw it away? Why betray everything you swore to serve?"

Ninety percent.

"Because what I swore to serve was a lie." Lucian kept his voice steady, buying seconds with words. "Because the system I believed in is designed to create suffering, not prevent it. Because I watched a man have his mind destroyed by people who call themselves protectors, and I realized that the only way to protect anyone is to stop them."

"The MNA commander. Speaks-Low." Kellam's expression shifted. "You were there. You saw what the Choir did."

"I heard it. I heard him breaking, night after night, until there was nothing left to break." Lucian felt the rage he had suppressed for weeks rising to the surface. "That is what we are. That is what we have become. A society that destroys minds to extract information, that builds weapons to devastate civilians, that tells itself it is the victim while it plans atrocities."

Ninety-five percent.

"And you think sabotaging the Nullwave will change that?"

"I think it will save lives. Thousands of lives, maybe more. I think that is enough." Lucian met Kellam's eyes. "I know you are going to arrest me. I know what happens next. But the code is almost uploaded. By the time your technicians find it, by the time they purge the corruption and restore the original programming, the deployment window will have passed. The MNA will have time to prepare. The attack will fail."

One hundred percent.

The console chimed softly. Upload complete.

Lucian smiled. It was not a happy smile. It was the smile of a man who had made his peace with consequences.

"Too late, Major. Whatever you do to me now, it is already too late."

Kellam stood motionless for a long moment. His hand remained on his weapon. His eyes moved from Lucian to the console and back.

Then he did something Lucian did not expect.

He took his hand off his weapon.

"I was at a frontier settlement once," Kellam said quietly. "Years ago, before I transferred to Intelligence. There was a sickness. We did not have the medicine to treat it. Children died. Families were destroyed. I requested emergency supplies and was told that resources were allocated according to priority, and frontier settlements were not a priority."

Lucian felt something shift in the room. The dynamic he had expected, the arrest and the interrogation and the execution, was not happening. Something else was.

"My sister," he said. "She died the same way."

"I know. I read your file." Kellam moved to the console,

studying the upload confirmation. "I have been building a case against you for months. And every piece of evidence I found made me wonder if I was on the right side."

"Major..."

"The Nullwave will kill thousands of people. Civilians. Children. People who have nothing to do with the politics that created this conflict." Kellam turned to face him. "I told myself that was acceptable. That our survival required hard choices. That the enemy would do the same to us if they could."

"But?"

"But I watched Speaks-Low too. I heard what you heard. And I realized that we are not making hard choices. We are making easy choices and pretending they are hard. It is easy to destroy. It is hard to build. And everything we do, everything our leaders plan, is about destruction."

Kellam pulled out his own data chip and inserted it into the console.

"What are you doing?"

"Adding redundancy." His fingers moved across the interface. "Your corruption will be found eventually. My contribution will make it harder to remove. Two sets of errors are more difficult to purge than one."

Lucian stared at him. The man who had hunted him for months was now standing beside him, sabotaging the same weapon, making the same choice.

"Why?"

"Because you were right." Kellam finished his upload and removed the chip. "Because the only way to protect anyone is to stop them. Because I am tired of being part of something I cannot believe in."

He moved toward the door, then paused.

"We have three minutes before the distraction response concludes and normal patrols resume. I suggest we both be somewhere else by then." He glanced back. "I will file a report saying I found the control room secure. You were never here. Neither was I."

"Major. Kellam." Lucian struggled to find words. "Thank you."

"Do not thank me yet. We are both dead if this is discovered. We are both traitors now." Kellam opened the door. "But at least we are traitors together."

He disappeared into the corridor. Lucian waited thirty seconds, then followed, walking back the way he had come, past guards who did not question him, through doors that opened at his touch, out into the night air of a city that did not know how close it had come to committing an atrocity.

The Nullwave was corrupted. The deployment would fail.

And somewhere in Nova-Providence, another man had crossed a line that could not be uncrossed.

The war was not over. But tonight, at least, the worst had been prevented.

Tonight was enough.

21

The Face of Betrayal

The trap had been set for three days when the answer came.

Aiyana had delivered the false intelligence personally, meeting with each Council member in private sessions that Chogan had arranged under the guise of security briefings. To Elder Makya, she had described a planned raid on the Untethered compound, complete with fabricated details about timing, approach routes, and the forces that would be deployed. To Councilor Waya, she had described a secret alliance with the Untethered, including false specifications of the countermeasures being integrated into the eastern network.

Both had listened with appropriate concern. Both had asked questions that suggested engagement with the material. Both had thanked her for the briefing and promised to keep the information confidential.

One of them had lied.

The confirmation came through channels that Tavani had helped establish: a network of informants inside the Pale Cities who monitored Choir communications. The message was brief but devastating.

Choir discussing MNA alliance with rogue faction. Countermeasure specifications received. Adjusting deployment parameters.

The countermeasure specifications. The alliance with the Untethered. The information Aiyana had given to Councilor Waya.

Not Makya. Waya.

Aiyana stood in Chogan's quarters, holding the message, and felt the world restructure itself around a truth she had not wanted to find.

"It makes sense," Chogan said quietly. He sat in his chair by the window, looking older than she had ever seen him. "Her advocacy for war. Her constant pressure to escalate. If she is working for the Pale Cities, her goal would be to push us into a conflict we cannot win. To exhaust our resources. To make us destroy ourselves."

"But why?" Aiyana heard her own voice as if from a distance. "She is one of us. Her nation has suffered more from Pale City aggression than almost any other. Her family..."

"Her family was divided." Chogan's voice carried the weight of knowledge he had carried alone. "Her mother was MNA. Her father was a Pale City defector who came to us thirty years ago. He brought intelligence that helped us for a time. But he also brought something else: a daughter who grew up between two worlds, never fully belonging to either."

"You knew this?"

"I knew the history. I did not know what it meant." He stood slowly, moving to face her. "Waya's father died when she was young. An accident, we were told. But there were always questions. Rumors that he had been discovered passing information back to his original contacts. That his death was not an accident at all."

"You think she blames us."

"I think grief makes people do terrible things. I think a child who lost her father might have been vulnerable to people who offered her answers, who told her the MNA was responsible, who gave her a way to channel her pain into purpose." Chogan's eyes were heavy with sorrow. "I think we failed her, long before she failed us."

Aiyana thought about the Council sessions she had witnessed. Waya's passionate speeches about defending their people. Her fury at every Pale City provocation. Her demands for action, always action, pushing against the restraint that defined MNA policy.

All of it a mask. All of it designed to make her look like the fiercest defender of MNA interests while she worked to destroy them from within.

"What do we do?"

"We cannot arrest her. Not yet." Chogan began to pace, his exhaustion momentarily forgotten in the urgency of the situation. "If we move against her openly, her contacts in the Pale Cities will know they have been discovered. They will accelerate whatever plans they have. They will act before we are ready."

"So we do nothing?"

"We do something more difficult than acting. We wait. We watch. We feed her information that serves our purposes rather than theirs." He stopped pacing and faced her. "And we prepare for the moment when we can move against her without warning, without giving her time to alert her handlers."

"She will continue to betray us while we wait."

"She will betray information we choose to give her. Information that is true enough to be believed, but shaped to serve our needs." Chogan's voice hardened. "The Pale Cities think they have an asset inside our Council. Now we have an asset inside their intelligence network. We can use her to send messages they will trust, precisely because they come from a source they believe is reliable."

It was a cold calculation. The kind of thinking Aiyana had associated with Pale City strategists, not MNA elders. But she understood its logic. Understood that the game they were playing required moves that felt wrong in order to achieve outcomes that were right.

"The Untethered," she said. "Tavani needs to know. If Waya has been passing information about them, their security is compromised."

"Tell her. But be careful what else you share. We do not know how far Waya's network extends. There may be others we have not identified." Chogan touched her arm, a gesture of connection he rarely offered. "You have done well, Aiyana. You have found the face of our betrayal. Now comes the harder part: living with that knowledge while pretending you do not have it."

"I do not know if I can do that."

"You will do it because you must. Because the alternative is worse." He released her arm and turned back to the window. "Go. Tell the Untethered. Then return to your duties as if nothing has changed. The next Council session is tomorrow. Waya will be there. You will have to sit across from her and show nothing."

"And then?"

"And then we wait for the right moment. It will come. These things always do."

* * *

Tavani received the news in silence.

They stood in the Untethered compound's communication center, surrounded by equipment that hummed with frequencies the Council had never authorized. Aiyana had flown through the night to reach her, carrying information that could not wait for secure channels.

"Councilor Waya," Tavani said finally. Her voice was flat, controlled, but something burned behind her eyes. "The voice of action. The one who has been pushing for us to be legitimized, brought into the fold, given a seat at the table."

"You suspected her."

"I suspected everyone." Tavani moved to a console and began entering commands. "But yes. Waya was on our list. Her rhetoric was too perfect. Too precisely calibrated to appeal to people like us, to make us trust her, to position herself as our champion inside the Council."

"Why did you not tell me?"

"Because suspicion is not proof. Because I needed to be certain before I accused a Council member of treason." Tavani turned to face her. "And because I was not sure I could trust you. You came from the Council's world. You carried their assumptions, their loyalties. For all I knew, you were Waya's agent, sent to identify us so we could be destroyed."

The honesty was brutal but fair. Aiyana had walked into the Untethered compound as an outsider, had been shown their secrets, had been given their trust despite every reason for caution. Of course Tavani had wondered. Of course she had held back.

"And now?"

"Now you have brought me proof that confirms my suspicions. Now you have demonstrated that your loyalty is to the truth, not to the Council's comfortable illusions." Tavani's expression softened slightly. "Now I trust you. As much as I trust anyone."

"What will you do about the security breach?"

"Move. Immediately." Tavani gestured at the screens around them. "We have contingency locations. Sites that Waya does not know about, that were established precisely for this scenario. By morning, this compound will be empty. The Pale Cities will find nothing if they come looking."

"The countermeasures?"

"Will be relocated with us. The integration with the eastern network will proceed, but through different channels, different methods. Waya passed along specifications, but those specifications were incomplete. We held back the critical details, precisely because we do not trust anyone completely." A ghost of a smile crossed Tavani's face. "Paranoia has its advantages."

Aiyana felt a measure of relief. The betrayal was real, but its damage was limited. The Untethered's caution had protected them. The countermeasures would still function.

"There is something else," she said. "Intelligence from inside the Pale Cities. The Nullwave has been sabotaged. Our assets corrupted the targeting systems. When they deploy, the weapon will fail."

Tavani went very still. "When did this happen?"

"Last night. Confirmation came through this morning." Aiyana watched the information land, watched Tavani process its implications. "We have more time than we thought. The deployment will be delayed while they identify and purge the corruption. Days, at minimum. Perhaps longer."

"Days." Tavani turned back to her console, her fingers moving rapidly. "Days to complete our relocation. Days to finish integrating the countermeasures. Days to prepare for whatever comes next." She looked up. "This changes everything."

"It changes the timeline. It does not change the fundamentals." Aiyana moved to stand beside her. "The Pale Cities will still deploy eventually. Waya will still be feeding them information. The war is still coming."

"But we will be ready for it. More ready than we would have been." Tavani stopped typing and faced her fully. "The Council's asset inside the Pale Cities. The one who sabotaged the Nullwave. Do you know who they are?"

"No. Chogan keeps that information compartmentalized. Too valuable to risk."

"Wise." Tavani nodded slowly. "But tell him this: the Untethered are grateful. Whatever happens, whoever they are, they have bought us something precious. Time. And in war, time is the one resource you can never get back once it is spent."

Aiyana thought about Lucian Ford, whom she had never met, whose name she did not know. A man inside the enemy's structure, risking everything to prevent an atrocity. A traitor to his people who was also, in some sense, their truest defender.

"I will tell him," she said.

She left the Untethered to their evacuation and flew east toward the rising sun. Behind her, an entire community was packing their lives into transports, abandoning a home they had built over fifteen years, becoming ghosts once more.

Ahead, a Council session waited where she would have to look into the eyes of a traitor and pretend she saw nothing.

The game continued. The pieces moved. And somewhere in the distance, the storm that had been building for generations continued its slow approach.

But for now, for this moment, they were still alive.
For now, that was enough.

22

The Reckoning

The surveillance report was waiting on Drax's desk when she arrived at her office.

She had requested daily updates on Rowan Halding's movements, his communications, his meetings with anyone outside the normal channels of government. For three days, the reports had shown nothing unusual. The Prime Councillor attended his scheduled appointments. He spoke with the expected officials. He maintained the appearance of a leader focused on the crisis at hand.

Today's report was different.

She read it twice, her face betraying nothing, her mind cataloging implications and calculating responses. When she finished, she set the report down and sat in perfect stillness for a long moment.

Then she activated her secure communicator and summoned her most trusted operatives.

* * *

Rowan was in his private study when they came for him.

He had been reviewing the latest reports on the Nullwave

situation, the chaos that had erupted when technicians discovered the corruption in the targeting systems. The deployment had been pushed back at least a week while teams worked to identify and purge the sabotage. The Choir was furious. The Assembly was demanding answers. And somewhere in the midst of it all, Rowan had felt something he had not felt in years.

Relief.

The sabotage was not his doing. He had not yet acted on the communicator Marin had given him, had not yet passed along the information she had requested. But someone else had moved first, someone inside the system who shared his growing horror at what the Pale Cities had become. The Nullwave's delay meant lives saved. It meant time to find another way.

The door opened without warning. Four figures in the dark uniforms of the Doctrine Keepers' enforcement division entered, spreading out to cover the room's exits. Behind them, Julienne Drax walked in with the measured grace of a predator approaching trapped prey.

"Julienne." Rowan set down the report he had been reading, keeping his movements slow and deliberate. "This is unexpected."

"Is it?" She stopped in the center of the room, her eyes moving across his desk, his shelves, the personal effects that filled this space he had thought was private. "I would have thought you would be expecting this. Given recent events."

"I do not know what you mean."

"Of course you do." Drax gestured, and one of her operatives moved to a section of wall that held family photographs. He pressed something, and a panel slid open to reveal a hidden compartment. Inside was the communicator Marin had given him. "We have been monitoring your communications for some time. Not the official channels, of course. Those you have kept appropriately clean. But this..." She took the device from her operative and held it up. "This is not an approved piece of equipment, Prime Councillor."

Rowan felt the ground shifting beneath him. He had been careful. He had hidden the communicator in a place no one should have known existed. But Drax had resources he had underestimated, surveillance capabilities that reached even into the Prime Councillor's private spaces.

"Where did you get this?" Drax continued, her voice soft and dangerous. "Who gave it to you? And what have you been using it for?"

"I do not have to answer your questions." Rowan stood slowly, drawing on the authority that his position still theoretically granted. "I am the Prime Councillor. You answer to me, Julienne, not the other way around."

"You were the Prime Councillor." Drax's smile was cold. "As of this morning, the Assembly has been convened in emergency session. Director Vance has presented evidence of your communications with enemy contacts. General Thorn has agreed to assume temporary authority pending a full investigation." She stepped closer, her eyes holding his without flinching. "You are no longer protected, Rowan. Whatever you have done, whatever arrangements you have made with the MNA, it ends now."

The speed of it was staggering. In the span of hours, Drax had dismantled his position, assembled the evidence, convinced the Assembly to act. She had been preparing for this, he realized. Waiting for the moment when she had enough to move against him.

"This is a coup."

"This is the lawful removal of a compromised leader. The Assembly has approved it. The military has endorsed it. The people will be informed that their Prime Councillor was discovered to be in contact with enemy agents and has been placed in protective custody pending trial." Drax's voice carried no emotion. "You brought this on yourself. If you had simply done your duty, if you had supported the necessary measures instead of questioning and hesitating and undermining, none of this would have been necessary."

"Necessary." Rowan felt something break inside him, not fear but the last remnant of the loyalty he had felt for the system he had served. "You are going to kill thousands of people with your weapon, Julienne. You are going to start a war that will devastate both sides. And you call it necessary."

"I call it survival. The MNA will destroy us if we do not destroy them first. That has always been true. The only question is whether we have the will to act." Drax nodded to her operatives. "Take him. Secure facility. No communications, no visitors, no contact with anyone until I authorize it personally."

The operatives moved forward. Rowan did not resist. There was no point. He was one man against a system that had decided he was expendable.

But as they led him from his study, as he walked through the corridors of a government building that had been his home for decades, he thought about Marin. About the communicator that had been found but not yet used. About the information he had gathered in his mind but never transmitted.

Drax had the device. But she did not have what was in his head. She did not know what he had learned, what connections he had made, what understanding he had reached about the true nature of the conflict and the people who drove it.

If he survived long enough to speak, he might still be able to change something.

It was a thin hope. But it was all he had.

* * *

The Assembly chamber was full when Drax entered to address them.

Representatives from every district of Nova-Providence had been summoned for the emergency session, their faces showing varying degrees of confusion, concern, and carefully hidden calculation. The news of Halding's arrest had spread quickly, but the details remained unclear. They had come to hear Drax explain what had happened and what would happen next.

She took her place at the speaker's platform and waited for silence to fall.

"Representatives of the Assembly," she began, her voice carrying to every corner of the chamber. "I come before you today with news that is both disturbing and, I believe, ultimately clarifying. Our Prime Councillor, Rowan Halding, has been discovered to be in communication with agents of the Many Nations Alliance."

Murmurs rippled through the chamber. Drax let them subside before continuing.

"The evidence is conclusive. A communication device of MNA manufacture was found in his private quarters. Analysis of its transmission history reveals contacts with known enemy operatives over a period of several weeks. Prime Councillor Halding has been placed in secure custody and will face charges of treason against the Renewal."

"What does this mean for the Nullwave deployment?" The question came from Representative Marsh, a hawk who had long advocated for aggressive action against the MNA.

"The deployment proceeds as planned. The sabotage that delayed our timeline was likely connected to Halding's treachery; we are investigating that possibility. Once the corruption is purged and the systems are verified, we will strike." Drax's voice hardened. "The MNA has attempted to weaken us from within. They have failed. Their agents have been exposed, their sabotage will be repaired, and their people will face the consequences of their aggression."

"Who will lead us?" Another representative, this one more cautious. "With Halding removed, the chain of succession..."

"General Thorn has agreed to assume temporary authority as Military Governor. The transition will be seamless. Our government continues to function. Our resolve remains unbroken." Drax surveyed the chamber, meeting eyes, projecting certainty. "This is a moment of crisis, yes. But it is also a moment of opportunity. The weakness that allowed enemy influence to reach so high has been exposed. We can now excise it completely. We can build something stronger, something purer, something that will never again be vulnerable to the lies and manipulations of those who would destroy us."

She saw the effect her words were having. Fear and uncertainty transforming into righteous anger. Doubt becoming resolve. The natural human desire to believe that someone was in control, that there was a plan, that the terrible events of recent days had meaning and purpose.

"The Renewal continues," she concluded. "It has always continued, through every challenge, every setback, every attempt by our enemies to break our spirit. Halding's betrayal is painful, but it is not fatal. We will endure. We will prevail. And when the dust settles, we will be stronger than before."

Applause began, scattered at first, then building to a sustained ovation. Drax accepted it with appropriate humility, bowing her head, playing the role of reluctant savior that the moment required.

Inside, she felt nothing but the cold satisfaction of a plan coming together.

Halding had been an obstacle. Now he was removed. Thorn was a military man, focused on tactics, uninterested in the complexities of governance that Drax had spent decades mastering. He would be a figurehead while she held the real power.

The Nullwave would deploy. The MNA would suffer. And in the chaos that followed, the Doctrine Keepers would emerge as the only force capable of maintaining order, the only institution that had remained true while others faltered.

She had been building toward this moment for years. Every crisis she had managed, every narrative she had shaped, every compromise she had extracted from weaker leaders had been preparation for the day when she would finally have the power to act without restraint.

That day had arrived.

And nothing, not Halding's betrayal, not the MNA's sabotage, not the doubts of representatives who still believed in limits and laws, would stop her from seeing it through.

The applause continued. Drax stood at the center of it, accepting what she had always believed was rightfully hers.

Power. Finally, completely, without compromise.

The Renewal had a new master. And she intended to use it.

23

The Unmasking

The Council chamber had never felt so small.

Aiyana stood at the edge of the circle, watching the faces of the assembled leaders as Chogan delivered the news that would shatter whatever remained of their illusions. The coup in Nova-Providence. Halding's arrest. Drax's assumption of power behind a military figurehead. The Nullwave deployment, delayed but not prevented, now under the control of the most extreme faction in Pale City governance.

And then, the revelation that would cut deepest.

"We have identified the source of our intelligence failures," Chogan said. His voice was steady, but Aiyana could see the cost in the lines around his eyes, the tension in his shoulders. "The person who has been passing operational information to the Pale Cities. The traitor who contributed to the compromise of Commander Speaks-Low's mission and countless other operations."

The chamber was silent. Every eye fixed on Chogan, waiting for the name that would change everything.

"Councilor Waya."

The silence shattered into chaos. Voices rose in denial, in accusation, in the particular fury of people confronting a betrayal they had never imagined possible. Waya herself sat frozen in her seat, her face a mask of shock that Aiyana could not tell was genuine or performed.

"This is absurd." Waya's voice cut through the noise, sharp and controlled. "I have given my life to defending the Alliance. My nation has suffered more from Pale City aggression than any other. You cannot seriously believe..."

"We do not believe. We know." Chogan's interruption was gentle but implacable. "Three days ago, I authorized a test. False intelligence was provided to you and to Elder Makya, different information to each of you. Within forty-eight hours, the information you received appeared in Quiet Choir communications. The information given to Elder Makya did not."

"That proves nothing. Someone else could have..."

"No one else had access to both pieces of intelligence. No one else was in a position to know what you knew." Chogan stepped forward, moving into the center of the circle. "The test was designed to be definitive, Councilor. It was."

Waya's mask began to crack. Aiyana watched the transformation, the careful facade giving way to something harder, older, more honest. The face of a woman who had been hiding for a very long time.

"You think you understand," Waya said quietly. The chamber had fallen silent again, every ear straining to hear. "You think this is simple. A traitor among you, working for the enemy, undermining everything you have built."

"Is it not?"

"It is nothing so clean." Waya stood slowly, her movements

deliberate. Guardians around the chamber tensed, hands moving toward weapons. "My father came to you thirty years ago. A defector from the Pale Cities, bringing intelligence, seeking asylum. You welcomed him. You praised his courage. You used everything he brought and promised him a home."

"I remember your father," Elder Makya said softly. "He was a good man."

"He was a fool." The word was bitter. "He believed your promises. He believed he could build a new life here, that his past would not follow him, that the people he had betrayed would not reach across the border to take their revenge." Waya's eyes moved around the circle, meeting each gaze in turn. "He was wrong. They reached him. They killed him. And when your investigators concluded it was an accident, when your Council decided not to pursue the truth because it might complicate diplomatic relations, I learned what your promises were really worth."

"Waya..." Chogan's voice carried genuine sorrow. "We did not know."

"You did not want to know. That is different." She laughed, a sound without humor. "I was thirteen years old. I had lost my father to people your Council was too afraid to confront. And then they came to me. Not the Choir, not the Doctrine Keepers. Someone else. Someone who understood my grief and knew how to use it."

"Who?"

"I never knew their name. I never saw their face. Just a voice, reaching me through channels that should have been impossible, offering me a way to make the Alliance pay for what it had allowed to happen." Waya's voice steadied, the confession becoming something almost like relief. "At first

I told myself I was seeking justice. Then I told myself I was preventing a war that would destroy both sides. By the time I understood that I had become the very thing I hated, it was too late to stop."

"You could have stopped at any time." Aiyana heard herself speak, her voice harder than she had intended. "You could have come to us. Told us the truth. Asked for help."

"And been executed as a traitor? Watched my nation bear the shame of my betrayal?" Waya shook her head. "You do not understand what it is like to be caught in a current stronger than yourself. To make one choice that leads to another that leads to another until you wake up one day and realize you have become a monster."

"Commander Speaks-Low," Aiyana said. "He is gone because of you. His mind destroyed. His life erased. Do you understand what you helped them do to him?"

For the first time, something like genuine pain crossed Waya's face. "I never meant for anyone to suffer like that. I passed information about operations, about planning, about vulnerabilities. I did not choose who was captured or what was done to them."

"But you made it possible. You gave them the tools they needed." Aiyana stepped forward, her anger overflowing its bounds. "You sat in this chamber and argued for war, for action, for defending our people, while you were the reason they needed defending. Every death. Every failure. Every compromise we made because we could not trust our own security. That was you."

"Yes." Waya's voice was barely a whisper. "That was me."

The chamber was utterly still. Aiyana could feel the weight of years pressing down on everyone present, the accumulated cost of a betrayal that had shaped events none of them had fully understood.

"Take her," Chogan said quietly. Guardians moved forward, their hands firm but not rough. "She will be held securely until we determine what to do with her. And she will tell us everything she knows about her handlers, her communications methods, every piece of information she passed and when."

"I will tell you everything," Waya said as they led her away. "It will not help. The people I worked with are better at this than you are. They have been doing it for generations. They planned for the possibility of my discovery. Whatever contingencies they have, whatever moves they make next, I was never told enough to predict them."

The door closed behind her. The chamber remained silent for a long moment.

Then Elder Makya spoke, her voice carrying the particular authority of someone who had seen more than anyone else present.

"We have lost much today. But we have also gained something. Clarity. For the first time in years, we know the shape of our enemy. We know how deeply they have reached into our councils. And we know that whatever comes next, we face it without the poison of betrayal still working in our midst."

"The Nullwave," War Chief Tahoma said. "The coup. Drax's rise to power. What does this mean for the attack we have been preparing to survive?"

"It means the attack is coming faster and harder than we feared." Chogan moved to stand at the center of the circle, where tradition demanded he speak from. "The sabotage bought us time. The Untethered's countermeasures are being integrated. But Drax will not wait forever. She will repair the damage, verify the systems, and deploy. We have days, not weeks."

"Then we prepare for days." Elder Makya's voice was firm. "Evacuations from the eastern network. Redundant systems activated. The barrier the Untethered have built, tested and ready. We do everything we can in the time we have."

"And then?" The question came from a younger councilor, one Aiyana did not recognize.

"And then we endure." Elder Makya's eyes swept the chamber, touching each face with the weight of her years and her certainty. "We have survived everything they have thrown at us for generations. We survived the first Divergence. We survived the Long March. We survived a century of hostility and the constant pressure of a neighbor that wanted us erased from existence. We will survive this too."

"The question is not whether we survive," Chogan added quietly. "The question is what kind of society we are when we emerge on the other side. If we become what they are, if we abandon everything we believe in the name of victory, then we have lost even if we win. That is what we must guard against. That is the true battle."

Aiyana listened and felt something shift inside her. The anger that had driven her through weeks of hunting, the cold fury she had felt when confronting Waya, began to transform into something else. Not forgiveness. She was not ready for that. But understanding. Acceptance of a world that was more complicated than heroes and villains, more painful than she had wanted to believe.

Waya had been a monster. But she had also been a grieving child, manipulated by people who knew exactly how to use her pain. Both things were true. Both had to be held together.

The Council began to discuss specifics: deployment of resources, communication protocols, the coordination with the Untethered that would determine whether their defenses held. Aiyana listened, contributed where she could, played her part in the machinery of preparation.

But part of her remained elsewhere. Thinking about Speaks-Low, whose mind had been destroyed. About Waya, whose soul had been destroyed years before that. About all the damage that had been done by people who believed they were doing what was necessary.

The Nullwave was coming. The barrier might hold or it might not. Thousands might live or thousands might die.

But whatever happened, they would face it with clear eyes. They would know what they were fighting for and what they were fighting against.

That had to be worth something.

It had to be.

24

The Wave Breaks

The sky turned wrong at seventeen minutes past midnight.

Aiyana was at the eastern barrier when it happened, standing beside Tavani in the control center the Untethered had constructed in the three days since their relocation. Around them, banks of equipment hummed with frequencies that pushed the boundaries of what Bioweb technology could do, amplifiers and modulators and defensive systems that had never been tested against a full-scale attack.

Now they would find out if any of it worked.

The first sign was visual: a shimmer in the air to the east, like heat rising from summer ground, except it was winter and the air was cold. The shimmer spread, becoming a wall of distortion that advanced across the horizon with the inexorable patience of a tide.

"Contact," one of the Untethered technicians said, her voice tight with controlled fear. "Nullwave signature confirmed. They have deployed."

"Barrier status?" Tavani was already at the primary console, her hands moving across controls that responded to her touch like living things.

"Charging. Seventy percent. We need another two minutes."

"We do not have two minutes." Tavani's voice was calm, matter-of-fact. "The wave will reach us in ninety seconds. We deploy at whatever charge we have when it arrives."

Aiyana watched the shimmer approach through the control center's windows. It moved faster than it appeared to, the distortion eating distance with a hunger that seemed almost alive. Behind it, she knew, the Bioweb was dying. Every node, every connection, every living system that made MNA technology possible was being torn apart by frequencies designed to shatter the harmony that held them together.

Sitala pressed against her consciousness, the eagle's fear matching her own. Through their bond, Aiyana felt the wrongness of the approaching wave, the discord that made every instinct scream to flee.

Stay strong, she sent. *Whatever happens, stay with me.*

Always, Sitala replied. *Until the end.*

"Eighty percent," the technician reported. "Sixty seconds to contact."

"It will have to be enough." Tavani looked up from her console and found Aiyana's eyes. "Whatever happens in the next minute, know that we did everything we could. The barrier is the best we could build in the time we had. If it holds, we survive. If it does not..."

"It will hold." Aiyana did not know if she believed it. But she said it anyway, because someone had to.

"Thirty seconds. Eighty-five percent."

The shimmer was visible through the window now, a wall of distortion that rose from ground to sky, advancing with the inexorable momentum of something that could not be stopped, only endured.

"Twenty seconds."

Tavani's hands hovered over the activation controls. Around the control center, every person had stopped moving, stopped breathing, stopped everything except waiting.

"Ten seconds."

The wrongness was overwhelming now, pressing against Aiyana's senses like a physical weight. Through her bond with Sitala, she felt the eagle's agony, the discordant frequencies tearing at the connection that had defined both their lives.

"Now."

Tavani activated the barrier.

* * *

The world became sound.

Not sound as Aiyana had ever experienced it, not the harmonies of the Bioweb or the songs of living things or even the harsh noise of Pale City machinery. This was something else entirely: two opposing forces meeting in a collision that transcended physical reality and became pure frequency, pure resonance, pure conflict.

The Nullwave hit the barrier like a wave hitting stone. For an endless moment, everything was chaos: lights flickering, equipment screaming, people crying out as the frequencies tore through flesh and mind. Aiyana felt her consciousness fragmenting, her sense of self dissolving into the noise, the bond with Sitala stretching to its breaking point.

And then, gradually, impossibly, the chaos began to recede. The barrier held.

Not perfectly. Not completely. Aiyana could feel damage spreading through the eastern network, nodes failing, connections severing, the Bioweb's song becoming ragged and uncertain. The barrier had absorbed the worst of the Nullwave's energy, had redirected and dispersed it, but some had gotten through. Some always would.

But the catastrophic collapse they had feared, the complete destruction of everything the eastern network supported, that had not happened. The barrier had done what it was designed to do: it had turned a killing blow into a wound.

"Status report," Tavani said. Her voice was hoarse, her face pale, but she was still standing, still in command. "All stations."

Reports came in from across the network, a patchwork of damage and survival. Nodes 7 and 12 had failed completely, their systems overwhelmed despite the barrier's protection. Node 15 was damaged but functional. Node 23 had somehow emerged almost untouched. The pattern was random, dependent on factors no one had been able to predict: local geology, the precise frequencies of each node's harmonics, simple luck.

"Casualty reports from the settlements?" Aiyana asked. Her voice sounded strange to her own ears, distant and uncertain.

"Coming in now." One of the technicians, his face gray with shock. "Medical facilities in sectors 7 and 12 have lost power. Environmental systems are failing. We have reports of injuries from equipment malfunctions throughout the zone."

"Deaths?"

"Unknown. Too early to tell." The technician swallowed. "But the evacuations. Most people in the highest-risk areas were already relocated. The Council's preparations..."

"Saved lives," Tavani finished. "The evacuations, the redundant systems, the barrier. All of it together. We lost less than we would have. Much less."

Aiyana moved to one of the windows and looked out at the

night. The shimmer was gone, the Nullwave's energy spent against the barrier's defenses. But the landscape beyond was changed. Where the Bioweb's harmonics had once filled the air with subtle life, there was now a kind of silence, an absence that pressed against her senses like weight.

They had survived. But they had also been wounded. And wounds, she knew, had consequences that took time to reveal themselves.

"What now?" she asked.

Tavani joined her at the window. "Now we rebuild. Now we strengthen the defenses that held and repair the ones that failed. Now we prepare for the possibility that they will try again."

"Will they?"

"Drax will not accept failure easily. She has staked everything on this weapon. When she learns that it did not achieve its intended destruction, she will look for ways to try again." Tavani's voice was matter-of-fact. "But she will also face consequences. Resources spent. Political capital exhausted. Questions from the people she has told that victory was assured."

"The sabotage helped," Aiyana said. "The corruption in their targeting systems. It weakened the wave, made it less focused than they intended."

"It did. Whoever our asset inside the Pale Cities is, they bought us the margin we needed." Tavani turned away from the window. "We owe them our survival. All of us."

Aiyana thought about Lucian Ford, whose name she still did not know. A man who had risked everything to corrupt a weapon that could have destroyed thousands. A traitor to his people who had saved hers.

The categories were becoming meaningless. Traitors and loyalists. Enemies and allies. Everyone was just people, making choices in circumstances they had not created, hoping the consequences would be something they could live with.

"I need to report to the Council," she said. "They will want to know what happened here."

"Go. We have things under control." Tavani's hand touched her shoulder briefly. "You did well, Aiyana. You held the pieces together when they could have fallen apart. Whatever comes next, remember that."

Aiyana nodded and walked out of the control center, into the night air that still tasted of discord and damage. Sitala was waiting for her, the eagle's presence in her mind battered but unbroken, their bond stretched but still intact.

We survived, Sitala sent.

We survived, Aiyana agreed. *But it is not over.*

It is never over, Sitala replied. *Until it is.*

They flew west together, toward Wakana Station, toward the people who were waiting to hear whether the world had ended or merely changed. Behind them, the eastern network flickered and struggled and slowly, painfully, began to heal.

The Nullwave had broken against them. Not cleanly. Not completely. But enough.

For now, enough was everything.

25

The Morning After

Drax received the report in her private office, alone.

She had sent everyone away hours ago, preferring solitude to the anxious faces of subordinates who did not know what to say. The Nullwave had deployed on schedule, the systems verified, the targeting confirmed. Everything had proceeded exactly as planned.

And it had failed.

Not completely. The reconnaissance drones that had followed the wave's path showed damage to the eastern MNA network. Nodes destroyed. Systems disrupted. The kind of harm that would take months to fully repair. By any conventional measure, the attack had been a success.

But Drax had not built the Nullwave for conventional success. She had built it to shatter the MNA's infrastructure so completely that they would never recover. To demonstrate, once and for all, that the Pale Cities could not be resisted. To break their spirit along with their technology.

Instead, the MNA had survived. Had somehow erected defenses that absorbed the worst of the attack. Had shown that their technology could evolve, could adapt, could meet threats that should have been overwhelming.

The reconnaissance reports mentioned something else. A barrier of some kind, generating frequencies that had interfered with the Nullwave's propagation. Technology that the MNA's official programs had never developed. Technology that came from somewhere outside their normal channels.

The Untethered.

Drax had known they existed. The intelligence from the broken MNA commander had confirmed their presence, their capabilities, their potential threat. But she had underestimated them. Had believed they were a fringe element, tolerated by the Council but not truly integrated into MNA defenses.

She had been wrong. And the cost of being wrong was everything she had worked for.

The Nullwave program had consumed vast resources. Political capital. Industrial capacity. The faith of Assembly members who had believed her promises of decisive victory. All of it spent on a weapon that had wounded but not killed, that had demonstrated Pale City aggression without demonstrating Pale City superiority.

The questions would come. They were already coming. Representatives demanding explanations. Military commanders wanting to know why their intelligence had been so incomplete. Ordinary citizens wondering why the great weapon they had been promised had produced results so far short of what they had been told to expect.

Drax would have to answer those questions. Would have to spin failure into a narrative of partial success, of lessons learned, of the need for continued resolve. She had done it before. She could do it again.

But something had shifted. She could feel it in the quality of the silence around her, in the looks she had seen on the faces of her subordinates before she sent them away. The aura of invincibility she had cultivated for decades had cracked. People were beginning to wonder if she was as infallible as she had always claimed to be.

She activated her secure terminal and began composing the messages that would shape the narrative. To the Assembly, emphasizing the damage inflicted on MNA infrastructure. To the military, ordering analysis of the barrier technology for future countermeasures. To the Signal Mesh controllers, preparing the public messaging that would transform defeat into a story of ongoing struggle.

The work of propaganda never ended. Truth was whatever people could be convinced to believe, and belief could be manufactured like any other commodity.

But as she worked, Drax found herself thinking about Halding. About the questions he had asked in that final meeting before his arrest. About the doubt in his eyes that she had dismissed as weakness.

What if he had been right? What if the path she had chosen led not to victory but to exhaustion? What if the MNA could not be broken, only fought, and fighting without breaking meant fighting forever?

She pushed the thoughts away. Doubt was a luxury she could not afford. The only way forward was forward, and she would walk that path until it led somewhere or until she fell.

The messages went out. The narrative began to take shape. And in the morning, when the sun rose over Nova-Providence, the Signal Mesh would tell the citizens of the Pale Cities that their weapon had struck a mighty blow against the enemy, that victory was closer than ever, that the Renewal continued unabated.

They would believe it, most of them, because they wanted to believe and because believing was easier than asking questions.

But somewhere in the city, hidden receivers would be capturing a different message. Elias Harren's voice, reaching through channels Drax could not fully suppress, telling anyone who would listen that the official story was a lie.

The war of narratives continued. And for the first time in her long career, Drax was not certain she was winning.

* * *

In Wakana Station, the Council convened to hear Aiyana's report.

The chamber felt different now. Waya's seat was empty, her presence erased as if she had never been there. The remaining members sat with the particular alertness of people who had just learned that one of their own had been a traitor, each wondering, perhaps, who else might be hiding behind a mask of loyalty.

Aiyana stood in the center of the circle and delivered her account. The Nullwave's arrival. The barrier's activation. The damage that had been sustained and the damage that had been prevented. The current status of the eastern network and the estimates for recovery time.

When she finished, the chamber was silent for a long moment.

"How many dead?" Elder Makya asked. Her voice was steady, but her eyes held the weight of knowing that the answer would haunt her.

"Forty-seven confirmed. Another thirty-two missing, presumed dead." Aiyana had memorized the numbers, had repeated them to herself during the flight back, trying to make them feel real. "Most were in the areas served by nodes 7 and 12, where the barrier's coverage was weakest. Medical facilities lost power. Environmental systems failed before backup could be restored."

"Seventy-nine." Makya closed her eyes briefly. "Seventy-nine people who woke up yesterday with lives and families and futures."

"Without the barrier, without the evacuations, without the sabotage that weakened the wave, the number would have been in the thousands." Chogan's voice was gentle but firm. "We mourn the dead. But we also acknowledge that our preparations saved lives. Many lives."

"The Untethered's barrier," War Chief Tahoma said. "It performed as they claimed it would?"

"It performed better than they had any right to expect." Aiyana thought about Tavani, about the years of work that had gone into technology the Council had refused to develop. "Eighty-five percent charge. Ninety seconds of warning. And it held. Not perfectly, but enough."

"Then perhaps it is time to acknowledge that we have been wrong about them." Makya opened her eyes, her gaze sweeping the chamber. "The Untethered have saved us. Their methods have proven themselves. Whatever philosophical objections we have had to their approach, the results cannot be denied."

"They still built weapons," another councilor objected. "They still pursued paths we explicitly forbade. Success does not justify..."

"Success justifies nothing. It only changes what is possible." Chogan stepped into the center of the circle, standing beside Aiyana. "The Untethered broke our rules. They also saved our lives. Both things are true. The question is what we do now, not whether we approve of how we got here."

"What do they want?" Tahoma asked.

"A seat at this table." Aiyana answered before Chogan could. "Recognition. A voice in the decisions that shape our future. They want to stop hiding and start participating."

"And in exchange?"

"They continue to do what they have been doing. Developing defenses. Building countermeasures. Preparing for the next attack that the Pale Cities will inevitably launch." She paused. "They are not asking us to change who we are. They are asking us to accept that who we are must include the capacity to defend ourselves."

The debate continued, as debates in this chamber always did. Voices rose and fell, positions clashed and found unexpected alignment, the slow work of consensus grinding forward through disagreement. Aiyana listened, contributed where her experience was relevant, and felt the particular exhaustion of someone who had seen too much in too short a time.

But beneath the exhaustion, something else was growing. A sense that the world had shifted, that the old categories no longer applied, that whatever emerged from this crisis would be different from what had come before.

The Nullwave had failed to destroy them. But it had succeeded in changing them. The MNA that would face the next attack would not be the same MNA that had faced this one. Whether that change was for better or worse remained to be seen.

The Council session ended as dawn broke over the grandmother oak. Decisions had been reached, compromises negotiated, a new path forward sketched in the uncertain light of morning. The Untethered would be invited to send representatives. Their technology would be integrated into official defense planning. The barrier would be strengthened, expanded, made ready for whatever came next.

Aiyana walked out of the chamber and found Sitala waiting for her on the branch where the eagle always perched during long Council sessions. Through their bond, she felt her companion's weariness matching her own, and beneath it, something that might have been hope.

It is over? Sitala asked.

This part is over, Aiyana replied. *The next part is beginning.*

Will it be better?

I do not know. Different, certainly. Maybe better. Maybe worse. Aiyana stroked the eagle's feathers, feeling the bond between them pulse with the familiar warmth that had sustained her through everything. *We will find out together.*

They flew out over the forest as the sun rose, leaving behind a Council that was still debating and a world that was still healing and a future that remained stubbornly uncertain.

The Cold War continued. The quiet border remained quiet, for now. And somewhere in the space between nations, the seeds of whatever came next were already beginning to grow.

26

What Remains

The investigation into the Nullwave sabotage began three days after the failed deployment.

Lucian had expected it sooner. Had spent the first forty-eight hours in a state of sustained tension, waiting for the knock on his door, the summons to an interrogation room, the moment when everything would unravel. But the knock never came. The summons never arrived. And gradually, impossibly, he began to understand that he might actually have gotten away with it.

The investigation focused on external penetration. The working theory, promoted by Director Vance and endorsed by Drax herself, was that MNA agents had somehow infiltrated the Nullwave facility and corrupted the targeting systems. Security protocols were reviewed. Access logs were examined. Personnel were questioned about unusual activities in the days before deployment.

No one thought to look for traitors within. The possibility was too destabilizing, too threatening to the narrative of unified purpose that held the Pale Cities together. It was easier to believe in enemy infiltration than in domestic betrayal.

Kellam's report had helped. The Major's official account described finding the control room secure during the distraction response, with no signs of unauthorized access. His credibility was unquestioned, his loyalty unimpeachable. If Kellam said the facility was clean, it was clean.

Lucian saw him occasionally in the corridors of the facility where both still served. They never spoke beyond what duty required. But sometimes their eyes would meet, and in that moment of contact, Lucian would see something that looked like understanding. Two men who had crossed a line together and found themselves on the other side, still alive, still serving, still waiting for whatever came next.

The message from the underground arrived a week after the deployment, carried through the dead drop he had used so many times before.

The barrier held. The damage was contained. Thousands live because of what you did. You have earned more than we can ever repay.

Lucian read the message in the privacy of his quarters, then burned it as protocol required. But the words stayed with him, warming something that had been cold for a very long time.

Thousands live. He had spent years wondering if anything he did mattered, if the information he passed ever made a difference, if his betrayal of everything he had been raised to believe served any purpose beyond his own conscience. Now he knew. The abstract had become concrete. People were alive who would have been dead. Families were intact who would have been shattered. A future existed that would have been erased.

That was worth something. That was worth everything.

He composed a reply, brief and careful as always.

Still in position. Ready for whatever comes next. The work continues.

He placed the message in the dead drop and returned to his duties, wearing the mask of a loyal officer who served the Renewal with unwavering dedication.

The mask was heavier now. But he had learned to carry it.

* * *

In the tunnels beneath Nova-Providence, Mira gathered what remained of the underground network.

The raids that followed Elias's escape had been devastating. Safe houses compromised. Members arrested or scattered. Communication channels disrupted. For weeks, the network had operated in survival mode, each cell isolating itself to prevent further damage, trust becoming a luxury no one could afford.

But networks were resilient. They had been building this one for years, with redundancies and contingencies designed for exactly this scenario. The core had survived. The mission continued.

"The Nullwave failed." Mira addressed the dozen faces gathered in the abandoned maintenance chamber, their features lit by the glow of emergency lanterns. "The MNA's defenses held. Drax's great weapon wounded but did not kill."

Murmurs rippled through the group. Hope and caution in equal measure.

"What does this mean for us?" someone asked.

"It means the narrative Drax has built is cracking. She promised decisive victory. She delivered partial damage." Mira's voice carried the controlled intensity that had made her an effective leader. "People are starting to ask questions.

Not many. Not loudly. But questions are dangerous things in a society built on certainty."

"Elias's broadcasts are helping." This from a young woman named Sera, who had joined the network only months ago. "My neighbors. They heard the latest one. They did not believe everything he said, but they listened. They discussed it afterward, when they thought no one could hear."

"That is how it starts." Mira nodded. "One conversation at a time. One doubt at a time. We cannot tear down the Signal Mesh overnight. But we can plant seeds in the cracks. Given enough time, enough persistence, those seeds will grow."

"Do we have time?" another voice asked. "Drax will try again. She will build another weapon, launch another attack. And next time, the MNA might not be able to stop her."

"Maybe. Probably." Mira did not believe in false comfort. "But Drax's position is weaker now than it was before the deployment. Resources are limited. Political support is eroding. Every day she spends rebuilding is a day we can use."

"And Halding?" Sera asked. "There are rumors that he has been moved. That Drax is planning something."

Mira's expression shifted, something darker moving beneath the surface. "Halding is beyond our reach. Whatever happens to him, we cannot prevent it. But his arrest has had unintended consequences. People who trusted him, who believed he was a good leader, are wondering why Drax moved against him. Some are starting to question whether the official story is true."

"Could he become a symbol? Like Elias?"

"He already is. Not to the masses, not yet. But to the people who knew him, who worked with him, who saw the man behind the position." Mira paused, choosing her next words carefully.

"Drax thinks she removed a threat when she arrested him. She may have created something worse: a martyr in the making."

The meeting continued, logistics and planning and the careful allocation of resources that kept a resistance movement alive. Mira guided the discussion, assigned tasks, maintained the discipline that had preserved them through the worst of the crackdowns.

But part of her mind was elsewhere. Thinking about Elias, safe now in MNA territory, his voice reaching across the border to plant doubt in the minds of people who had been raised on lies. Thinking about Lucian, whose name she did not know, still inside the system, still working, still risking everything.

Thinking about her mother, who had disappeared so long ago for the crime of telling the truth.

The work continued. It always continued. That was the only answer to despair she had ever found: keep working, keep building, keep believing that the small acts of resistance would someday add up to something larger.

The meeting ended. The members dispersed through tunnels that had hidden generations of truth-tellers, returning to lives of quiet deception where they waited for the next opportunity to act.

Mira remained behind, alone in the darkness, listening to the silence of the deep earth.

The Nullwave had failed. The barrier had held. And somewhere in the cracks that were opening in the Pale Cities' certainty, seeds were beginning to grow.

It was not victory. It was not even the beginning of victory. But it was something. And something, after so many years of nothing, felt like everything.

She extinguished her lantern and walked into the darkness,

following paths she knew by memory, returning to the surface world where she wore a different face and played a different role.

The tunnels swallowed her footsteps. The silence returned.

And in the depths where light never reached, the network continued its patient work, waiting for the day when the world above would finally be ready to hear the truth.

27

The Quiet Border

One month after the Nullwave, Aiyana returned to the border.

Not to the eastern network, where repair crews still worked to restore damaged nodes and refugees were slowly returning to homes they had been evacuated from. Not to Wakana Station, where the Council continued its debates about integration and defense and the shape of a future no one could predict. She returned to the frontier itself, the no-man's-land between nations, where the quiet that gave this conflict its name was most profound.

The observation post was a small structure grown into a hillside overlooking the border zone. She had served here once, years ago, before the Wind Spine incident, before everything had changed. In those days, she had been a young Guardian learning to read the patterns of movement across the divide, watching for signs of incursion or opportunity.

Now she was something else. She was not certain what to call it.

Sitala circled overhead, riding thermals that rose from the warming earth. Spring was coming to the frontier, the long winter finally releasing its grip. In a few weeks, the trees would bud and the grass would green and the land would pretend that nothing had changed, that the world was the same as it had always been.

But everything had changed. Aiyana could feel it in the Bioweb's altered harmonics, in the conversations she had with leaders who looked at her differently now, in the weight of knowledge she carried about traitors and allies and the thin margins that separated survival from catastrophe.

She had come here to think. To find a moment of stillness in a life that had become defined by motion.

The border stretched before her, invisible but real, a line drawn by history and maintained by fear. On one side, the living forests of MNA territory, their systems slowly healing from the damage the Nullwave had inflicted. On the other, the industrial smog of the Pale Cities, visible even from here as a gray haze that stained the eastern horizon.

Two worlds. Two futures. And between them, a silence that was not peace but merely the absence of open war.

"I thought I might find you here."

Aiyana turned. Chogan stood at the entrance to the observation post, his travel cloak dusty from the journey. He looked tired, as he always did now, but there was something else in his expression. Something that might have been hope.

"You tracked me," she said.

"I asked Sitala." He smiled slightly. "She is easier to find than you are."

He moved to stand beside her at the window, looking out at the same view she had been contemplating. For a long moment, neither spoke.

"The Council has made its decision about the Untethered,"

he said finally. "Full integration. A seat at the table, as they requested. Tavani will represent them."

"That is good." Aiyana meant it. Whatever reservations she still held about the Untethered's methods, the barrier had proven their value. And Tavani, for all her intensity, was someone who could be worked with.

"There is more. The Council has created a new position. Liaison between the official Guardian structure and the Untethered. Someone who can move between both worlds, coordinate operations, ensure that integration happens smoothly." Chogan turned to look at her. "They want you to fill it."

Aiyana was silent for a long moment. The offer was not unexpected, not after everything she had done in recent weeks. But hearing it made it real in a way that anticipation had not.

"I am twenty years old," she said. "Six months ago, I was an engineer who had never seen combat. Now you want me to bridge two factions that have spent fifteen years in opposition?"

"I want you to continue doing what you have already been doing. You found the Untethered. You negotiated with Tavani. You carried terms between factions and helped build the alliance that saved us." Chogan's voice was gentle but firm. "Age is less important than experience. And you have gained more experience in the past months than most Guardians gain in a lifetime."

"Experience in what? Hunting traitors? Watching people I trusted reveal themselves as enemies?" The bitterness surprised her, rising up from somewhere she had not known it was hiding. "I have learned that nothing is what it seems. That everyone has secrets. That the line between ally and enemy is thinner than I ever imagined."

"Yes." Chogan nodded slowly. "That is exactly what you have learned. And it is exactly what you will need to navigate what comes next."

Aiyana turned back to the window, watching Sitala wheel against the pale spring sky. Through their bond, she felt her companion's steadiness, the eagle's simple certainty that they would face whatever came together.

"What does come next?" she asked.

"Drax is already rebuilding. Our intelligence suggests she is developing a second Nullwave, learning from the failures of the first. The Choir is recruiting new technologists. The border incidents are increasing, probing attacks testing our defenses." Chogan's voice carried the weight of someone delivering news he wished he did not have to share. "The Cold War is not ending. It is intensifying."

"Then why does the Council want integration? Why bring the Untethered into the fold now?"

"Because we cannot afford division anymore. Because the next attack will be worse than this one, and we need every capability we can muster. Because the old ways of doing things, the careful separation between official policy and unofficial action, nearly killed us." Chogan moved to sit in one of the observation post's worn chairs. "The Council has finally understood what the Untethered understood years ago: we are in a war, whether we call it that or not. And wars are not won by pretending they do not exist."

Aiyana thought about Speaks-Low, whose mind had been destroyed. About Waya, whose soul had been destroyed long before that. About Lucian and Kellam, whose names she did not know, sabotaging weapons in facilities she would never see. About Elias, broadcasting truth into a society built on lies.

About Mira, leading a resistance in tunnels beneath a city that wanted to erase her.

All of them soldiers in a war that had no front lines, no clear enemies, no victories that were not also defeats.

"I will do it," she said. "The liaison position. I will take it."

"I knew you would." Chogan's smile was tired but genuine. "You are not someone who walks away from responsibility, no matter how heavy it becomes."

"That is not a compliment."

"No. It is a burden. But it is also who you are." He stood slowly, joints protesting. "I am returning to Wakana Station. The Council session resumes tomorrow. Will you come?"

"Soon. I need a little more time."

Chogan nodded, understanding without needing explanation. He touched her shoulder briefly, a gesture of connection, then walked out of the observation post and into the spring morning.

Aiyana remained at the window, watching the border, thinking about everything that had happened and everything that was still to come.

* * *

The sun was setting when she finally left the observation post.

Sitala descended to meet her, landing on an outcropping of rock that jutted from the hillside. Through their bond, Aiyana felt the eagle's quiet contentment, the simple pleasure of flying and hunting and existing in a world that asked nothing more complicated than survival.

She envied that simplicity, sometimes. But it was not her path.

We go back now? Sitala asked.

We go back, Aiyana confirmed. *There is work to do.*
There is always work.
Yes. There is always work. Aiyana stroked the eagle's feathers, feeling the bond between them pulse with warmth and strength. *But we do it together. That makes it bearable.*
Together, Sitala agreed. *Always together.*

They launched into the evening sky, rising above the border, above the divide that separated two worlds locked in a conflict that had no end in sight. Below them, the frontier stretched in both directions, a landscape of possibility and danger, of histories that could not be undone and futures that remained to be written.

The Nullwave had failed. The barrier had held. The traitor had been exposed. The alliance had been forged.

But none of it was over. The Cold War continued, deeper and more dangerous than before. Drax was building new weapons. The MNA was integrating new allies. And somewhere in the space between them, people on both sides were making choices that would determine whether the next crisis ended in survival or catastrophe.

Aiyana flew west, toward Wakana Station, toward the Council chambers where decisions waited to be made, toward a future she could not predict but would help to shape.

Behind her, the border remained quiet. The silence held.

For now.

Author's Note

This novel imagines a world that never was: a North America where Indigenous nations formed a continental alliance, where colonial settlement unfolded under Indigenous authority, and where two radically different societies now face each other across an ideological divide. It is speculative fiction, rooted in a simple question: What if history had bent differently?

The Many Nations Alliance depicted in these pages is a fictional composite. It draws inspiration from the philosophies, governance structures, and ecological relationships of numerous Indigenous cultures across North America, but it does not represent any single nation, tribe, or tradition. The technologies, rituals, and social structures of the MNA are inventions of this story, extrapolated from real principles of reciprocity, balance, and environmental stewardship that many Indigenous cultures share, but shaped into something new for the purposes of this narrative.

I want to be clear about what this book is and is not. It is not an attempt to speak for Indigenous peoples or to represent their lived experiences. It is not a claim to cultural knowledge I do not possess. It is, instead, an act of imagination that takes seriously the idea that other ways of organizing society, technology, and humanity's relationship with the natural world are not only possible but have always existed alongside the path Western civilization chose to follow.

The animal bonds portrayed in this story are meant as relationships, not magic. They require work, mutual respect, and ongoing consent from both partners. No character is born with an innate right to such a bond; they are earned through patience and attunement. I have tried to ensure that these relationships never imply genetic superiority, spiritual entitlement, or abilities unavailable to others through different paths. If I have fallen short of this intention anywhere, the failure is mine alone.

The Pale Cities, too, are a fictional creation. They are not meant as a direct allegory for any particular nation or political movement, though readers may find resonances with various historical and contemporary societies. The people who live within them are not villains by nature; they are people shaped by the stories their culture tells, struggling to survive within systems they did not build and may not fully understand. The conflict at the heart of this series is ideological, not ethnic. It is a collision between ways of seeing the world, not between peoples who are inherently good or evil.

I am grateful to the scholars, writers, and knowledge keepers whose work has shaped my understanding of Indigenous history, philosophy, and resistance. Any wisdom in these pages is borrowed; any errors are my own. I have tried to approach this material with humility, curiosity, and respect, knowing that imagination is not the same as knowledge, and that fiction, however well-intentioned, cannot substitute for the voices of those whose ancestors actually lived these alternatives.

This story asks what might have been. It does not presume to say what should be, or to speak for those who continue to carry forward the traditions, languages, and wisdom that colonialism tried to erase. If this novel inspires readers to seek out those voices directly, to learn from Indigenous writers, historians, and communities in their own words, then it will have accomplished something worthwhile beyond entertainment.

Thank you for reading.

www.ingramcontent.com/pod-product-compliance
Lightning Source LLC
LaVergne TN
LVHW041910070526
838199LV00051BA/2566